The FANTASTIC FABRICATED LIFE OF LYLE FARKER

THE FANTASTIC FABRICATED LIFE OF LYLE FARKER

KAYLEIGH MARINELLI

atmosphere press

For my Poppy and all his endless stories

THE REVENGE OF
KAREN'S CHILI

The cat clock's tail above the desk sways back and forth with a rhythmic precision that radiates a hum with the beat of my chest. The ticking fills the silence as Dr. Calian drags his hands across his bald head as if he were trying to read my fortune. The sour tang of my armpit finally reaches my nose and my nostrils flare up in defiance. I am wet with sweat and I cannot stop my fingers from shaking.

Finally, Dr. Calian meets my eyes. I try to read him; try to pull back on his stone-cold psycho-therapist exterior and get into the guidance counselor side of him—his softer side. I always thought he spent more time at the school as a counselor than in his office as a therapist, but in a small town like Crooks, Wyoming, it makes sense that he would be both.

I can't read him. He lets out a sigh in tune with the clock. Balance, I think. Balance in the chaos.

"Lyle, you better have a good reason for sneaking into my office and going through my things. And using my telephone!" His voice inflects, and I try not to flinch. I drag my hands through my messy, unbrushed hair and allow the sweat to tame my locks. I watch as Dr. Calian recomposes himself, sitting up straighter and leaning on his elbows closer to me. "Lyle, I am going to hear you out here. Give me one good reason why I shouldn't bring this to the principal and have you expelled. And right before graduation!" I swallow and play with the frayed strings of my sweatshirt. I rushed too quickly out of the house to be bothered with grabbing a jacket.

"It's a long story," I admit, hoping that Dr. Calian will send me on my way. Hoping he won't make me relive all of the pain I've been through for the past five months.

"Luckily for you, I have time to listen." Dr. Calian folds his hands properly. I try to do the same in my lap—anything to stop the shaking. My fingers twine together in a sacred protection only the mummified pieces of gum underneath the table can see. I take a deep breath and let it release from my nose.

"Honestly, it all started with Karen's chili," I say. Dr. Calian squints his eyes but doesn't say anything. This is my cue to continue. Tell him everything, I think. Tell him every lie, every meltdown, every moment. It's time for the truth.

FIVE MONTHS AGO

When I came home from school the first Friday of winter break, I found Karen in the kitchen blasting Duran Duran and sweating into the chili. She gets home from the bank early on Fridays, and always makes it a point to try a new meal with lean meat and organic veggies. The week before she made a delicious stew, one that filled my tummy with love and warmth. A warmth much needed during the cold in January.

Ever since I told Karen that I had dreams about Larry as Godzilla—long tail, scales, and sonic breath—terrorizing our refrigerator, going through the drawers and shelves with veracity and starvation, she has tried to enforce a healthy diet. And, although I do love clementines, I just cannot force myself to swallow a mouthful of brussels sprouts. She thought a healthy diet would lead to a healthy lifestyle and I would no longer be dreaming of my dead father as a monster.

But, it didn't work. No matter how many times I ate those clementines, I still had those monster-Larry dreams, dreams that the five grief counselors I have been to haven't been able to stop either.

The song switched from "Rio" to "The Reflex" and Karen started adding an assortment of beans into the chili—kidney, black, pink, and others. The music was loud enough that she didn't hear me come in.

"Karen," I said, trying to out-pitch the music. "School sucked today." She still couldn't hear me though and continued to sway back and forth. "Karen!" The sultry vibes of the lead singer were too much for me to compete with, I was outmatched. "Mom!"

"What!?" Karen snapped around, dropping a can of beans onto the floor. "God damnit, Lyle. Don't sneak up on me like that! Now we are only going to have a six-bean chili." Karen moved to the pantry and pulled out the broom and dust pan, sweeping the beans into it quickly.

"Did you say something about school?"

"No, Karen, nothing about school." I left Karen to her cleaning and low-fat cooking to escape into my bedroom.

Karen often called my room "the aftermath of Hurricane Lyle" which I thought was insensitive, but I forgave her due to the generation gap. All of my t-shirts existed in the Northeast Kingdom of my room. My shoes resided under my bed with empty chip bags infested with dust, and Greg, the monster who lived there and used to tickle my feet when I was little. Karen thought I should have outgrown an "imaginary friend" by now, but Greg insisted that he was real.

My pants have, more or less, managed to stay in the closet; but, I've always thought that hangers made it suffocating for my pants. Plus, hangers cause wrinkles, and how was I supposed to look classy with wrinkles?

I went to the Northeast Kingdom and dug through it to find a plain black t-shirt that seemed fancy enough to wear to a party—the party I still had to convince Karen to let me attend. I stopped fussing about my shirt—I was sure that someone would wind up spilling a beer on me and black felt like the most appropriate color to absorb whatever gross beer was going to be served at this party. I am a wine man myself. And by wine I mean grape juice. I don't like drinking because it makes my mind funny.

I looked at myself in the mirror and thought, for a moment, that I could be a strapping young lad who could snatch up all the ladies with my slick black hair and intoxicating blue eyes. Dark hair and blue eyes much similar to that of Larry's. That's why I avoid mirrors. That way I didn't have to see him. Plus, brushes were evil. Girls liked a more natural look anyway, right?

I went into the kitchen to savor Karen's chili and find a way to tell her that I would indeed be skipping out on the *Star Wars* marathon tonight to attend a high school party. Usually I would be wolfing down this chili. The back of my throat would burn as I tried to swallow too many meat chunks—man the taste was sensational. But all I could do was push my spoon around the bowl. Karen gave me the stink eye before clearing her throat in a dramatic manner.

"Lyle."

"Karen."

"Mom. It's supposed to be Mom."

"Right. Mom."

"Is there something wrong with your chili? You've barely touched it." She looked at me with her 'I'm concerned, and you better answer me' eyes. "Do you need me to call Dr. Calian and set up a Saturday appointment?"

"No, Karen, this isn't a Dr. Calian thing, this is an, Allen asked me to go to this party with him and he bribed me with Spider-man comics and The Rib and Chop house, and I couldn't say no because he is my best friend, thing." I gave her the best half-assed smile I could muster while thinking about my earlier conversation with Allen during school that day...

* * *

Mr. Metters droned on in the background about a county project while fighter jets were attacking each other right outside the window. I could smell the fiery tang of gasoline as each jet blew by me, leaving my hair in cosmic disarray. They were fighting for the title of champion. Each jet set out to beat the other in a fast-paced death race outside of Harper K-12.

This reminded me of the first time I saw a tree morph into a bionic robot shooting acorns while I was sitting in social studies a couple of months after Larry died. This tree was the size of a house and tore up the school playground across the street. It was almost like the playground was a bowl of spaghetti and the bionic tree was starving. Soon after that, the jets became a regular occurrence.

One of the jets traveled quickly to the ground and

exploded into the colors of red and electric blue when a "pssst" rang into my ears, pulling me from my vision.

I looked over to see Allen staring at me.

"I have a proposition for you." He looked to the front of the classroom and back in a dramatic motion, 'to build suspense' he would say. "I'm talking capital D for Dangerous proposition. Becky is having a party tonight; we should go."

"No, I will not go with you so we can loiter by the punch bowl and eat all the sour cream and onion chips like last time."

"I just got the new Spider-man comic." Damn. He knew the way into my heart.

"Go on," I said. His smile grew into full mania.

"Come with me to this one party and it's yours." I stroked my chin in an equally dramatic manner. I want to stir his pot a little. See what else he would offer me.

"I'm considering it." His smile didn't give as he leaned in closer to me. His scrawny body hung out in the alley between desks in a way that I was sure Metters would notice but ignore for as long as possible.

"And a trip to Texas Roadhouse. On me." Damn times two. He won. Time to up the ante.

"Make it The Rib and Chop House and you got yourself a deal. But I'm bringing my own chips this time, the ones from the last party you dragged me to tasted like soap." He threw his fist in the air and made a giddy noise, fully alerting Metters to our position.

"Lyle Farker and Allen, are you listening to me?"

"Aw, how come you didn't say my last name?" Allen complained as Metters snorted the air like a line of cocaine.

"I said you're in a project group with Ellison and Becky. You have to find something historical and interesting about our county to do a project on."

"What?" Allen looked like a loopy dog after a vet visit. He even had one tooth sticking out past his lip. Maybe he would attack Metters and pee on his leg so we didn't have to do this project at all.

"I just said it, Allen, but I will repeat it again just for you. You and your group will get together after school—I know, tragic and time consuming—but you must research a historical event from our county and do a report on it. It can be a myth, but you have to prove why it was a story and how it impacted Crooks County. Easy. Pay attention next time, Allen." I stifled a laugh into my sleeve and Allen groaned.

"Now we have to go to Becky's party. How else are we going to find out anything interesting about this damn county?" Allen huffed while slumping down into his chair.

"Allen, save your comments for later." Metters' final comment made the class erupt into laughter. Allen's cheeks were red as cherries.

I noticed Becky's smile aimed at Allen, and for a second I thought that she might actually have stars in her eyes, but realized that it was the reflection of the gray trash can beaming off the semi-clean floor and assaulting her eyes with dust particles.

Allen never questioned my way of seeing the world. In fact, he would always talk about how he wished that he saw bionic trees that destroyed teachers' cars. Especially old Ms. Peterson who didn't let him go to the bathroom one time in second grade, so he shit himself and was called Poop Pants for the rest of the year. This memory made me smile as Allen curled into himself from embarrassment.

* * *

My memory was interrupted by Karen scolding me. "Lyle, you shouldn't be going to parties at all, and you certainly shouldn't let Allen bribe you. Do you remember what happened last time?" She leaned forward into her chili trying to threaten me further with her stink eye.

"Yeah, the all you can eat pancakes at the diner and I had to go to the hospital because I chugged a whole thing of syrup and got a stomach ulcer." I remembered that day well. All the nurses were practically lining up at my room to get an autograph. I was a celebrity in that wing.

"And why did you chug the whole thing of syrup?" I convinced myself that she was going to high dive into her chili if she got any closer to it.

"Cause Allen told me if I did it he would give me his limited edition, non-opened Luke Skywalker action figure. But I still want to go to this party. I owe my friend and plus Dr. Calian is always telling me to engage in my social life more instead of my fantasies."

"Well, Lyle." Game, set, and match, I had her now.

"I have to go. Plus, I already have my bag of sour cream and onion potato chips ready." Karen knew how I felt about my chips. Larry's favorite snack. It would devastate her to say no to me now.

"Fine, but home by 11 and lights out by 11:30." Karen slurped her chili up. It took me a minute to realize that she actually just said yes.

"Deal! Thanks, Karen." I dug my spoon into my chili and began shoveling it into my mouth. It was delicious. I indulged in every bite before leaving for the party.

* * *

A couple of hours later, I decided to walk to Becky's house in case I got too wild at the punch bowl. Becky's place was only a couple of blocks away from mine, and I never minded a stroll dimly lit by flickering street lights which made the shadows of the road appear to be darker than they really were. It made me feel like I was in an action movie and I could be attacked at any moment by velociraptors. The lamp posts acted as a forest of trees that were hiding these prehistoric creatures. Each time I passed one, it was like I was getting through a checkpoint in a videogame that I was playing with myself. It felt exhilarating. Crazy, but exhilarating. The road slushed from the snowfall that we had the week before. My shoes kept making a slushy-squeal each time I took a step which reminded me that winter was still in full force.

When I arrived at Becky's an abundance of people were pouring in and out of her front doors. No doubt her parents were away on a fancy vacation this weekend. Loud, obnoxious music assaulted my ears. I wanted to turn around and take my chances with the velociraptors, but I saw Allen waving at me with a bottle of vodka in his hands. I pulled my way through the people stampeding me like wild prehistoric animals trying to get to the house.

"Are you honestly going to drink that, or did you fill it with water like last time?" I pointed to the bottle of vodka he was swinging around like a knock-off Prada bag.

"You know I can't hold my liquor, Lyle, but this way no one harasses me for not drinking and I can stay hydrated throughout the night," Allen said while jiggling the alcohol bottle, the water sloshing back and forth inside. As far as anyone in the party was concerned, that was vodka.

"You're hilarious," I told Allen, who smiled at me. I pulled my shirt out from underneath my armpits. I was already sweating. There was something about being stuffed into someone's house with a bunch of drunk people that made me nervous. I never fit in at these things, but I wanted Allen to have a good time, so I was going to have to suck it up.

If the outside of Becky's house was a watering hole, then the inside was the forest from Jurassic Park. Kids were everywhere punching each other in encouragement to take another shot of chocolate whipped vodka, or they were pressed against the wall with tongues searching for each other like a lizard searching for flies. Allen and I almost had to fist fight a pack of female triceratops to get into the kitchen.

Now when I say that Becky's house looked like a Jurassic forest—that was exactly what it was. Trees to the ceiling thick enough that one would need a machete to get through the tangled vines and roots. A lingering stench of wetness—of death. In a world like that one, you were either the predator or you were the prey, and there the prey rarely survived. Behind every corner you never knew what you were going to find—would it be a group of kids playing a harmless game of pong, or would it be Derek, waiting, drool dripping down the front of his shirt because he was starving for a Lyle Sandwich? Every crack of a beer can opening sounded like the snap of a branch underneath the foot of a rabid predator. I refused to let myself be prey here—act cool, Lyle. Act like the predator and that was what you would become, right?

To my left, I watched in horror as a young meat-eating dino picked up an unknowing lizard and bit its head off. The head detached itself from the body and peeled back like a slice of cheesy pizza. Lizards were clearly the pizza of the Jurassic period, and every hungry dino was looking for an excuse to dig their claws into a snack.

To my right, a group of female veggie-eating dinos grazed peacefully and whispered gossip to one another. They were probably talking about which beefy jock dino was the hottest, or who was going to be the first person to pass out at this party. They wore a fashionable red lipstick color that smeared over their teeth. When they smiled you would think they ate carcasses, not leaves.

Thadeous was in the corner of the living room/forest jotting down some notes in his flip notebook. Thadeous and I weren't exactly friends; but, we always bonded over our hatred for bullies. I wondered what about this party had given him the sudden urge to write. I bet it was all the dry humping. He had excellent source material here for his story. I couldn't blame the guy for taking notes. Maybe he saw a forest too? I would never know the contents of his novel in progress.

Becky's large house seemed overwhelmed by the amount of students (and dinosaurs) here, which was funny considering we live in the smallest town imaginable. I secretly thought that Becky put an RSVP online and the entire state of Wyoming showed up tonight. There were plenty of people there who I had never seen before. That, or, I spent a lot more time in my imagination than I thought.

Once Allen and I got to the kitchen we settled into the party position. One hand held my sour cream and onion potato chips while the other remained in my pocket. This way no one could put a drink into my hands that I would have to evacuate into a plastic plant by the end of the night. I was not interested in drinking anything here. I scanned the crowd of Jurassic beasts when the alpha male appeared at the front door. *Derek.*

* * *

Earlier that day, Allen talked about wanting to do our project on the hobo graffiti artist who drew anatomically correct penises on buildings in the 1980s. Allen called him his artistic hero because anyone who can graffiti Optimus Prime's dick in the middle of town deserved a cape.

I was too busy thinking about Optimus Prime's dick slapping Megatron midfight. This triggered a huge earthquake that swallowed Megatron. This allowed Optimus to pride around town and get any of the ladies he wanted. My thoughts followed me as we went outside to go home and get ready for Becky's party. I heard the bustle and struggle of a freshman squirming as he was forced to lick chewing gum on the handrails by none other than Derek and his band of goons.

* * *

Now, Dr. Calian, you know Derek thinks he's hot shit because he can throw a football and count to seven. He's obnoxiously big so that makes it easy for him to pick on everyone else. His dad looks exactly like him which is uncanny. It's almost like they copied his father in a lab instead of Derek being born. That would make him a science experiment and not a human which was a soothing thought. Derek also recently lost a tooth. He tells people that it is from a time he hit someone so hard during a football drill that it popped his tooth out. I think he just doesn't brush his teeth.

Chard is the doofy one and just repeats everything Derek says in a less intelligible dialect.

He always manages to get a piece of wet lunch meat on his shirt that learns more about algebra than he does. He no doubt saves the meat for later, or lets his dog, Meatball, lick it off. He lives almost outside of town in a small cottage with his grandmother, whom I always thought was a witch. Their front lawn is always used as a garbage dump for kids, and the decorations usually include Bud Lite cans and Fireball bottles.

Ellison is smaller in stature and always wears a colorful button up shirt. He's wanted to go to Princeton since we were kids, and he recently got accepted. Ellison used to come over my house all the time in first grade after he and his family moved here from Baltimore City. We would smash peanut butter and jelly sandwiches while watching dinosaur documentaries. I don't know what he's up these days aside from following Derek around and preparing for college.

* * *

Anyway, continuing with the story—Derek stopped the forced licking to make eye contact with me and scoff with joy. His group floated over to us like a pack of judgmental flamingos. I could see the sweat gathering at the back of Allen's neck as the flamboyant birds perched in front of us.

"Where do you think you're going, Lyle Farter," Derek said while rubbing his tongue in the empty spot where his tooth should be.

"Ah, yes, Derek and his goons, just who I wanted to run into today. Let me ask you this, do you possibly think you can come up with a burn worse than 'farter'."

"Sometimes I forget how much of a smartass you are, farter."

"Yeah, tell'm, Derek," Chard chimed in a few seconds later. He was probably thinking about Meatball, or what he would have for dinner.

"Oh, Chard, I almost forgot you were standing there. Must be because you were supposed to graduate a year ago, but I suspect nothing less from the guy who abbreviates 'Richard' to 'Chard'."

"What the fuck did you just say?" I could see the steam seeping from Chard's ears when he closed the space between us and got up into my face.

"Do you need me to have it translated into dumb for you?" In another world Chard would've bit my head off, or at least spit on me, but in this world Ellison spoke up instead.

"Hey, Lyle, just cool it, yeah?"

"Your friends started it, and I have no problems ending it." Before any other words slipped from my mouth, Derek grabbed me by the collar and lifted me from the ground. It reminded me of the wedgies that he used to give me when we were little. They were so catastrophic that I would have to go home and sit on a bag of frozen peas and Larry would read old stories to me about plants who ate people.

"You better stay away from us and I better not see you anywhere near Becky's tonight.

Not that you would leave your house and your mommy and all the photos of your fatass dead dad anyway." Derek threw me onto the ground as he and his goons stalked off. His hips shook irreverently as he morphed back into a flamboyant flamingo. I hoped they encountered a pack of rabid dogs that thirsted for flamingo legs. That way they could never walk up to me and Allen like that again.

"Hey, don't listen to those guys. They have shit for brains anyway. Plus, your mom makes the best banana bread known to man and Mr. Farker always told us the best stories." Allen pulled me from the ground and patted my back.

"Yeah, you're right. Plus, I couldn't stop staring at all the rips in Chard's shirt. They looked like the map to Middle-Earth. It was super distracting," I said while trying to fix the collar of my shirt. Derek was able to actually rip the seams of my Ghostbusters shirt. He was going to pay for that. I've had this shirt since seventh grade—it was practically vintage.

"We're still going to the party, right?" Allen asked, smiling at me and batting his eyelashes all sexy like.

"You put comics and steak on the table. We're going. And I hope that Derek sees us there too." Allen and I split to go to our cars. The entire time I drove home I thought about Middle Earth, zombie flamingos, and Meatball. I might've rolled a stop sign or two. I forgot.

* * *

Obviously, Derek's threat wasn't enough to keep me

away from Becky's house, but right then the jungle and my throat seemed to be closing in on me. I wasn't sure how someplace that was already claustrophobic could become immensely smaller in the fraction of a second—how the presence of one person could make you go from feeling like a top predator to a snack.

I looked to Allen who was busy having eye sex with Becky from across the room. She was even coming over here, no doubt to steal his alcohol. Her long blonde hair swayed back and forth like a shampoo commercial. If I was friends with her, I would ask her what kind of conditioner she used, because even I could see the lusciousness.

But I had a bigger problem to deal with. I needed to get out of the kitchen before Derek found me. I stuffed my chips onto the nearest table and dashed upstairs for safety. I had to fight my way through more fornicating dinosaurs just to lock myself in the bathroom which acted as the only place of refuge in this jungle. I assumed that Allen would be okay with Becky. I knew a bedroom eye when I saw one. You should take notes here because shit's about to get serious.

I sat on the cover of the toilet seat and thought about making fart noises to make it seem like I was in there as an emergency. Then, my stomach actually started to growl. A warning.

Fifteen seconds until I actually needed to go to the bathroom. Karen's chili was kicking and screaming in my lower intestine while it wreaked havoc in my digestive track. Twelve seconds. I fumbled with my belt, forgetting which way I was actually supposed to pull it. Ten seconds. I finally jimmied my belt free and began to pull my jeans down to meet sweet relief. Six seconds. I grabbed onto my boxers like a child would grab a puppy and just yanked.

The revenge of Karen's chili began before I was even able to fully sit down onto the toilet. I could hear the gross sloshing sound of my desecration hitting the water. But this sounded more like a thud than a splash. I gasped in relief. But something wasn't right. It didn't sound right.

Alarms began to sound off in my head. I was lounging on the toilet fifteen seconds ago. I didn't lift the lid. I looked back to see what looked like a mud derby spun out by a muscle truck splattered onto the lid of Becky's toilet seat. I looked around to see what I could possibly do to rectify (no pun intended) this situation.

I could feel little bits sticking to the back of my legs. I waddled over to the sink and grabbed a hand towel. I wet it quickly and dragged it across the back of my legs and butt. I was afraid to look at the towel. The tangy smell of beans and beef was enough for me to know that I had gotten myself into quite the pickle. I finally pulled my pants up and looked at the rest of that mess.

In my eighteen years of life, I had never seen something quite like this before. But then I could see the true power of Karen's chili. I couldn't help but be impressed. But it was not the time to ogle over my Jackson Pollock bathroom explosion. I needed to clean this up somehow.

I considered swiping the entire roll of singly-ply toilet paper but didn't want to risk making the mess worse. I settled on a decorative hand towel sporting a majestic bird. I began to wipe it up in a sloppy manner. I would have to throw the towel out discreetly downstairs, along with the one I used to wipe my legs. Everything was going according to plan. I was going to be able to hide this.

Then I heard the door handle jingle and a knock fell onto the door.

If this was a horror movie extending from me successfully surviving the walk over here, the other side of the door would house the bloodthirsty velociraptor ready to extract revenge. My chances of making it into the third act were slim. I was either going to get eaten or have to jump from a second story window and break both my legs when I hit the ground and desperately crawl a few inches, before being eaten. Either way I was dinner, and I'm probably fucking delicious.

I finally gathered my bearings to face the velociraptor. There was no way in hell I was going to die in a toilet like the lawyer from *Jurassic Park*.

"It's occupied." Another knock fell on the door.

"Occupied." This time the knock that followed was aggressive. The velociraptor must have been hungry.

"Jesus Christ, can a man shit in peace?"

"Lyle, is that you?" I heard from the other side of the door just before the raptor burst through it.

It turned out that the bloodthirsty velociraptor was actually worse. Derek. There was a strange look on his face. One that read: *I actually have no idea what's going on here because I killed my last good brain cell smashing head first into someone else's bathroom door.* His smile was wide and gross though. Probably because he let the stench out into the hallway.

Derek tried to charge me but lost his balance, causing him to slip in some of the revenge of Karen's chili that I missed when wiping up the floor. He slid around in it like a fish flopping on a deck before finally falling into it butt first. Luckily, he wore white pants, so the brown stained his back side beautifully. I could see it seeping into his thighs. Derek must have been drunk because it took him a moment to stand up. Then he put his hand right into another section of puddle that I forgot to wipe up and I had to suppress a laugh.

I used that moment to escape into the hallway before a group of jungle creatures looked in on the crime scene I created. It sounded like hyenas giggling before someone chimed in, "No way! Derek shit all over the bathroom!" I wasn't sure why I was thinking about hyenas in that moment—they didn't even live during the same time as the dinosaurs. I tried not to read too much into it the inconsistencies in my projected imagination and looked into the bathroom to see that Derek's rear end was indeed stained; he looked like the culprit of the situation. I was able to slide out just in time. The hyenas roared with laughter as I continued my escape downstairs. If I stayed there any longer it would look suspicious.

I returned to my spot by the punch bowl which was abandoned by Allen. I looked around the party and saw that everyone was much drunker than when I went upstairs. I could tell because people were puking everywhere. Aimee Sharp threw up in the trash next to me. Normally I would think that was disgusting, but I used this moment to throw out the two towels I was hiding behind my back. This way the stench of the puke would at least mask the poop. I loitered there for a few more minutes hoping that Allen would return and we could leave.

I took in big gasps of breath, ones that made it feel like I needed to get out of here. The forest that was Becky's house existed inside my chest now and there wasn't enough room in my sternum to house the traumas of the past. I abandoned waiting for Allen and headed straight for the door. Unfortunately, Derek made it there a moment before me.

"I know it was you, farter." Derek put an accusatory finger to my chest. He slurred his words and I could smell him. Or me; I guess.

"I have no idea what you're talking about," I lied, praying that no one else saw me up there. Praying that Derek didn't punch me in the face right then. I dug at my armpits again, a reflex, to make sure that no one could smell my fear.

"You're the only shithead here that could have produced that much feces. I don't know how I'm gonna prove it, but I will." The group of hyenas that laughed at Derek upstairs made their way into the kitchen and continued to make fun of him.

"I'm impressed that you know the word feces," I said, watching as the group of hyenas continued to grow and turn their attention to the giant stains on Derek's pants. Derek covered himself up. There was no way he was going to be able to say anything about me here. Not with half the school in the kitchen staring at the massive poop stains that littered his pants.

"Screw you, farter." Derek and Chard strolled off toward the exit of the house. As Derek walked away, I saw that the back of his legs was not only stained, but there were multiple plump bruises there. One was even shaped like a dog's face, which was equally amusing and concerning. Those bruises must have been from football, right? But the season ended already so that didn't make any sense.

The hyenas were quick with their gossip because everyone was pointing and laughing as they left. Ellison lingered behind for a moment. Maybe he knew that it was me in the bathroom, too? How was I going to get myself out of that one if he knew?

"He's really not that funny, is he?" Ellison adjusted a button on his shirt without making eye contact with me while he spoke.

"No, he's more like a half-funny ape." I was still stuck on his threat. Derek could be real scary sometimes. I remembered when a kid took his seat in class. Derek gave the kid the worst wet willy. The kid got an ear infection from it; but the school couldn't prove Derek did it because the teacher was facing the board. The last thing I needed was a lethal wet willy. But at least Ellison didn't know it was me in the bathroom. My social destruction was put on hold.

"Yeah, you're right," Ellison agreed but didn't elaborate. He just continued to stare at me, and I was starting to feel awkward. What was I supposed to say to him anyway? I didn't even know if he liked the same things as when we were little. I could ask him how his little brothers are doing, but to be honest I don't remember their names. So, I was stuck there just staring too.

"Hey, have you thought of anything to do for our history project?" Ellison asked, dragging on our conversation. All I could think about right then was getting home and taking a shower.

"Allen mentioned wanting to do the graffiti artist from the 80's. You know, the one who spray painted all the dicks?" I said, trying to suppress the disgust I felt over the idea. Ellison gave me a weird look. Since he was going to Princeton, he was going to want to do something more vigorous than that. "I know—I'll think of something better than that," I said, mentally promising myself that there was no way I was going to let that be our research project for the rest of the year.

"Cool. See you Monday, Lyle." Ellison left to reunite with his crew. It came to my attention that Allen probably wasn't going to be coming back, and I was no longer interested in eating my sour cream and onion potato chips. Somehow, they were spoiled by the entire situation I had put myself through, and I really needed to get out of there. All I needed was one more person to find out the truth about the bathroom, then life would be over for me.

I left out the back door and saw Allen laying in the grass with Becky looking up at the stars. He murmured something about celestial whales as Becky stared at him like he could be the only boy alive. Maybe seeing her staring at him in class with loving eyes wasn't a fluke. Maybe popular girl Becky Road really did have a crush on glasses wearing, star obsessed, future astronomer, Allen Parson.

I left them to talk about the sky and started to head back home. No velociraptors followed me, but Larry did. He walked side by side with me, except he was a T-Rex. A big one. The one from *Jurassic Park*.

He wore a windbreaker jacket—red, white, and blue—just like the one Larry used to wear when he was alive. His little arms barely stuck out past the sleeves. The dark brown and green scales looked wet with either sweat or condensation that seeped off the asphalt. He swayed back and forth, and with each new step I felt the vibrations underneath my feet. If T-Rex Larry wasn't careful, he would open up the earth below me and I would be swallowed whole.

He didn't say anything or look at me. He simply kept walking at my pace as the street lights flickered ominously. I seriously needed to stop watching so many horror movies. But what was more concerning was seeing Larry. Well, T-Rex Larry. Why was this happening to me? I usually only saw him in my dreams, but that? Was there something wrong with me?

T-Rex Larry tried to reach out and grab my hand, but he couldn't reach. His arms were too small and he was too far away.

When I finally got home, I found Karen sitting at the kitchen table. She didn't scold me, rather she just let me slip by. I was about to head upstairs to take easily the most refreshing shower of my life but decided to turn around and talk to her.

"Did you eat all of the sour cream and onion chips?" Karen asked, giving me the Mom look that screamed that she wanted all the dirty secrets from the party. Little did she know.

"You know me and my chips, Karen. They never survive the night." That was my chance to escape her line of questioning, but before I could get away, she added—

"How was the party?" Well, let me see, Karen. *It was going great until your chili made me shit all over the place,* I thought. But I probably shouldn't say that out loud. If I did Derek might somehow hear me and that would fuel his revenge fire. And I couldn't even think about telling her about seeing T-Rex Larry. Then she would really think that I was crazy.

"Great, I can't wait to go again." I started to nervously play with the hem of my t-shirt. "Oh, and hey, can you call Dr. Calian? I would like to converse with him tomorrow." Karen fully looked me in the eyes. She wore a different kind of expression then. An expression that fell somewhere between concern and acceptance. I knew that Karen wouldn't ask questions about me talking to Dr. Calian—she had been trying to get me to talk to him again for years—but I also didn't want to tell her about seeing Larry IRL. I knew I should at least talk to Dr. Calian about it—see what he thought about the situation.

"Of course, darling." Karen didn't question me as I dashed upstairs. Praise. I took my shower, entered the barrage of hurricane Lyle, and poured myself into bed. The image of T-Rex Larry walking with me burned.

"How am I going to get myself out of this one?" I said aloud. That truly was a shitty situation to be in. Although having seen my dead father as a Cretaceous beast was concerning, at least I knew I wasn't alone. That was how I was going to get through it. With T-Rex Larry.

If only I could see the future.

SCHOOL GUIDANCE COUNSELOR SESSIONS **AREN'T VANILLA**

Karen dropped me off at school on Saturday to visit Dr. Calian during his weekend office hours. She was probably going to do mom things like grocery shopping where she would run into an old friend and talk about nothing for hours. That would mean I would be stuck there longer. The thought of that was honestly excruciating. At that time, I hadn't been to Dr. Calian's office in a long time, but I still remembered where it was—all the way down the hall on the left close to the first graders' classrooms. The worst part of going to a K-12, honestly, is all the screaming first graders.

When I went inside, he wasn't there. On his desk was a picture of his three young daughters and wife. Everything was in pristine shape. He was stunningly organized. I felt like I was the dirt that follows Pig Pen, from Charlie Brown, around, and if I moved around too much in the seat all of my stank would get everywhere and taint his office.

I thought about rummaging through his things to see where people like Derek were considering going to college. Probably a dumpster large enough to stuff an entire football field in. Just when I was about to sleuth, Dr. Calian walked in looking as dapper as ever. That was the first time I thought about going through Dr. Calian's things, but I didn't. I swear. At least not yet.

Dr. Calian was never one for small talk. He liked to get right to it. He sat in his chair and stared at me for a minute. He looked straight into my face, straightened some already straight papers, and dove right into our appointment.

"It's been quite a while since you last came to see me, Lyle. What has changed your mind about coming in for weekly sessions?"

"Well, I figured that it would be good for me to talk to someone. Plus, your office always smells like vanilla, and it reminds me of these bomb ass cookies my mom used to make when I was little." I thought about telling Dr. Calian about seeing T-Rex Larry last night, but then he would start asking a bunch of questions I didn't know the answer to. Maybe coming here was a mistake. "Also, I may or may not have made Derek angry and he scares me."

"What do you mean?" Dr. Calian looked up right away. He had a concerned look on his face that made me nervous.

"Well, you know Derek. Always a hot head. And I may or may not have embarrassed him in front of the whole school at a party last night," I admitted, but casually left out the fact that the embarrassment I was talking about involved him being covered in shit—literally.

"Well, Derek is focusing on maintaining his scholarship, so I highly doubt that he has time to worry about what other students think about him, Lyle. So that should ease your worries for a little bit." I wanted to believe Dr. Calian, but I seriously thought he was underestimating Derek's ability to be a butthole. I was just going to have to keep my distance. "Derek aside, what was going to this party like for you?" Dr. Calian leaned forward rubbing the black stubble on his chin.

"I mean. Good? I don't know how to handle parties. There is too much going on." *And all the students are savages,* I thought.

"Did you have fun?"

"Not really," I said while shifting to stuff my hands into my pockets to play with the lint. "Allen left me to hang out with—well, someone else." I could hear that my tone of voice was borderline whiney and I needed to tone down the dramatics a bit. I didn't want Dr. Calian to know how much I really needed Allen to be there.

"You remember what I told you before? About always relying on one person?" Dr. Calian asked.

"Yeah, but he has always been there for me, ya know? And I have no way of knowing if anyone else would ever be as reliable as Allen. Plus, he understands the way I see the world and all." Dr. Calian scribbled in his pad. I hate when people do that during meetings. It makes me feel like they are writing a prescription, or worse, writing down jokes about me to tell to colleagues later. Something like "this kid is such a loser he only has one friend." And well, if that wasn't the truth.

"Since you brought up your own imagination, Lyle, when was the last time you saw Larry in your dreams?" Dr. Calian continued to scribble and, in turn, I continued to sweat.

"Two nights ago."

"And was he a creature again?"

"As always." *A big juicy T-Rex,* I thought. But he was also a big, juicy, T-Rex last night, in the road, walking with me. But I still didn't mention that.

"Have you ever, in detail, spoken to anyone about the true nature of your father's death?" I brought my hands out from inside my pocket and started to wring out my hands on my lap. They were sweatier than I originally thought, which made me feel gross and uncomfortable. What was left of the lint balls were sticking to me.

"No, there's nothing to talk about." What was I supposed to say to people? Hey, my name is Lyle Farker, and I see my dad in my dreams as a fifty-foot slobbering demon monster, what's your name? Hell no. People would think I was crazy.

"You found him, didn't you?"

"Would now be a good time to mention that I love the smell of this office again?" I said—anything to change the subject at this point. I'd even talk about horse wangs for God's sake. But Dr. Calian kept staring at me, so I knew I would have to answer him soon. "Yes—have you been speaking to Karen?"

"Your mother is concerned about you, Lyle. She wants you to be able to discuss the trauma that you've experienced so you can adequately move forward with your life. Go to college some day and get out of Wyoming. She also spoke about you isolating yourself from your peers, is this true?"

"What? That's not true, I see Allen every day. And I just told you that I was at a party last night."

"Peers besides Allen. And you said you didn't enjoy the party, or is there something else that you aren't telling me about that?" Oh no. He knew all my secrets. I had to divert that conversation.

"I said hi to Thadeous. And Aimee."

"Well, that's good. Maybe you should hang out with them sometimes." I was stuck thinking about Thadeous talking about Dementors and Aimee talking about horses. I noticeably cringed at the thought. "Okay, I can see that is out of the question," Dr. Calian added before finally finishing up the novel he was writing in his pad.

"I want you to spend the day with someone who isn't Allen and every time you have a vivid daydream, I want you to write it down in a journal. Which means, yes, you will have to purchase a journal."

"Why do I have to write notes about my daydreams?"

"Writing will help you process your imagination on the page—to help you see what you are seeing in a different way, so to speak." Dr. Calian was going to kill me. He knew I hated English class. I wanted to throw myself out the window when we were reading *Romeo and Juliet*. "Also, I took the liberty of putting together some colleges for you to look into." Dr. Calian handed me a rather thick envelope that I could already tell is going to get sucked up in the hurricane of my room. "I want you to consider applying to some of these for creative writing.

You'll have to do some research, which means, yes, you will have to read."

"Don't be silly, Doc. You know I don't read." He glared at me. This man was consistent AND good at his job. Damn him. But he did explain himself well.

"But I don't want to hang out with anyone else. Or read."

"How do you know if you don't try? It is a solid start to move forward in your future and your recovery. Another thing you should consider doing is going into the room in your house that you spent the most time with Larry—allow yourself that. And before you argue about it at least consider. It is a healthy way to confront something that you have been avoiding for a long time." He had me there. I didn't have anything left to argue at that point. Hell, reading a book or two wouldn't kill me. Three though, three would kill me. The idea of going into my basement was uncomfortable though. I hadn't been down there in ten years. What if something had changed?

What if nothing had?

"Fine, but I'm going to be sassy about this, just prepare yourself." I pouted by crossing my arms in front of my face dramatically, mostly because I was trying to cover up my armpit stains. At the very least I could try to make him feel a little bit bad about making me do research and read.

"I go home to three young daughters every day, Lyle. I am well prepared for any level of 'sass' you throw at me. Shall we meet again next week?" I nodded at him while gathering together all the materials he gave me. Damn. He hadn't even budged at my dramatics. The man deserved an award.

I walked out of his office with thoughts flooding my head. Creative writing. Man, who was gonna read a book about a kid who sees lockers as demons that consume the souls of students? A deliciously fucked up person, that's who.

When I went outside, I saw Karen sitting in the parking lot blasting music and playing air guitar. It was embarrassing. Luckily, it was Saturday. And no one was around to bear witness.

Especially Derek. I poured myself into the car and Karen was giving me the look. The, *I wanna know what you talked about but won't invade your privacy*, look.

"Well?" She asked while lowering the music enough so she could hear my response. "Dr. Calian looks like he's lost some weight. I wonder if he's been using a Bowflex."

"Lyle."

"Karen, you know, perfectly well, the rules that surround doctor-patient confidentiality. I cannot speak to you about my appointment. Because, I am, in fact, bound by law. I do apologize for that, but I am happy to report that Dr. Calian's office still smells like vanilla. I almost had to stop myself from licking the walls."

"Lyle, that law is only in place for people who go to see therapists—not their school guidance counselors." I stared at Karen and refused to answer her. She may be right, but that didn't mean I was going to tell her anything about our meeting. After a painful moment of us just staring at one another, she finally folded and said, "I am just happy that you finally agreed to see him again."

"Well, you know what they say about when shit hits the fan? In my case it was a toilet seat, but I'm getting the same vibes here."

"What are you talking about?" I laughed to myself about the pun and Karen having no idea what I was talking about. Some things were better left in the bathroom.

"Ahem, doctor-patient confidentiality. And, hey, can you play that one song I like by Def Leppard?" Karen sighed at my failed comeback.

"Of course, sweetheart."

"Pour Some Sugar on Me" began to bump through our old jeep's sad speakers as we drove home. The birds flying by began to morph into pterodactyls. Maybe I should write this down? No, not yet. I'd let myself relish in the beauty of it one more time before I had to start documenting things.

I really did try to keep my thoughts under wraps—I

told myself that dinosaurs were extinct, that my classmates weren't actually rabid animals, and that my dad was gone and never coming back. The surrounding view opened up into the vast landscape of *Jurassic Park*. It was filled with beautiful dinosaurs grazing while others beat the crap out of each other.

A deep ephemeral moan of one of the large dinosaurs filled the stagnant air, alerting all of the others to its gargantuan presence. Each step it took was enough to shake the car from side to side. I looked to Karen to see if she was seeing this, but she continued to sway to the tunes of the car radio I had already forgotten about. It was easy for me to forget, especially when the world opened up before me, prehistorically.

It was easier that way, living inside my imagination all the time. And I am happy to say that it wasn't the end of the world.

The landscape surrounding us began to be enveloped by the asteroid that killed the dinosaurs. For a moment my vision was blurred enough by red that I had to squint my eyes.

I couldn't help but laugh to myself and whisper: *Well at least not yet.*

REENTERING
🔲 PAST

When Karen and I got home, she continued her mom duties like sweeping and yelling on the phone with a mortgage company about some shenanigans. Normally, I would perch myself on the couch and watch a movie marathon or hang out with Allen, but I kept staring at the basement door. I hadn't been down there since the last Friday before Larry's death. I wasn't even sure if Karen had gone down there. But Dr. Calian did say it was a good time to go into that specific room—the room I had been avoiding.

An acidic bubbling began to assault the back of my throat. It tasted like Mountain Dew and I began salivating. If I spat right then it would burn holes in Karen's luscious curtains. I was becoming feral in my quest to continue staring at the basement door. Was it a good time to write in my journal? Right, I still need to pick one up. Maybe T-Rex Larry was trying to tell me something.

* * *

One time, when Larry, Allen, and I were watching *Jurassic Park* in the basement, Allen stomped around like the dinosaurs with a greasy slice of pepperoni pizza hanging out of his mouth. For me, *Jurassic Park* was sacred time. It was when I slurped on countless Mountain

Dews, ate an obscene amount of sour cream and onion potato chips, and Larry would always quote the movie behind me which would tickle my ears with excitement. My favorite was when he would scream "Clever Girl!" which he would follow with a demonic tongue flick while throwing his marshmallow fluff body around in a way that a s'more wouldn't appreciate.

Allen had brought jelly beans and shoved one so far up his nose that Larry had to pull it out with a pair of tweezers. Larry was holding Allen down as he was squirming.

"Alright, little guy, if you don't stop moving I'm going to accidentally pull out one of your nose hairs," Larry said as Allen started to cry hysterically.

"But, but—Mr. Farker! I don't want any nose hairs! I don't want to be a man yet! My dad said I have to pay bills when I'm a man, and I don't have any money!" Allen cried as Larry shoved the tweezer into his nasal canal. I watched from the corner, setting up the movie. Allen's little limbs flailed back and forth, and his black rimmed glasses fell to the floor. Larry finally got him to calm down by bribing him with gushers, which he also shoved up his nose.

* * *

I hesitated to go into the basement in that memory. It had been like "Caution" or "Police Line Do Not Cross" was slapped across the entrance of the basement for all these years, but then I was mentally tearing down those banners and replacing them with a huge neon sign saying, "ENTER HERE, LYLE." It felt almost like a message from the universe. Or a message from T- Rex Larry and Dr. Calian.

Either way, there was a sign—metaphorical not physical. I'd have to ask Karen about maybe putting up a physical sign though. A little fluorescent light in the living room could go a long way for the property value. Karen always said things like "light ambiance" and I am not totally sure I understood what that meant.

I finally pulled myself up from the couch and moved over to the entrance of the basement. I stood there for a minute before putting my hand on the knob. It was hot. In school they taught us that if a door is hot it means there is a fire on the other side of it, and we shouldn't open the door. I was going to be consumed by the fiery pits of hell anyway, so I opened the door. On the other side weren't flames and smoke, just the same staircase that had always existed there. I closed the door and began my descent.

I felt like an adventurer, after ten years. I was seeing the walls that I knew so well—eggshell not white (ambiance)—but they seemed alien somehow. The eggshell was discolored to an awful yellow. One that screamed neglect. One that I was sure didn't fall into Karen's aesthetic.

The actual basement looked the same. The same black leather couch that could double as a porn prop. The same big backed television set, dusty and worn. I could hear it whispering the sounds of the early 2000s. The same stack of VHS movies.

I rummaged through the eggcrate laying at the bottom of the stairs to the right. Inside it was a handful of plastic dinosaurs I used to play with when I was little. Phillip—my pterodactyl, was missing. Along with the dinosaurs was a crusty pair of tighty whities that had emblems from *Star Wars* on them. They were small enough to have fit my eight-year-old buns. I couldn't remember why they were left down here.

Maybe I stripped them and Larry yelled "Lyle, although we are indoors, we keep our clothes on in this house!" or "Lyle, how many times do I have to tell you that the floor isn't the bathroom!" Not that I pooped on the floor when I was little or anything—that was something I was prone to only in my adult years at parties, it seemed.

I tossed the undies back into the crate and continued looking around. I got down onto the floor and peered underneath the couch. I hoped there wasn't a couch monster that had been starving for the last ten years and was hungry for flesh. Luckily, there were only a bunch of crushed Mountain Dew cans and a mummified chip bag. I pulled the chip back out and peered inside. Along with the world's stalest chips, a cicada carcass was inside. I threw the chip bag back onto the floor and kicked it underneath the couch. I wasn't sure if the cicada was one- hundred percent dead, but I wasn't going to explore long enough to find out.

The only photo hanging on the wall was one of me, Larry, and his brother, Uncle Danny.

We were hanging out at some stream I forgot the name of, and we were all holding up the fish we caught. Both Larry and Uncle Danny were holding up sad little minnows, but I was holding a monster of a fish—one the size of my whole arm. I remembered almost having to give the fish an RKO to get it to calm down and smile for our picture.

Larry and Uncle Danny had scowls on their faces. They were joking about wanting to look disappointed by the size of their fish. It showed in the photo. My fish and I were the only ones smiling. I laughed at the memory. I hadn't seen

Uncle Danny since Larry died. I didn't even know where Uncle Danny was now.

I forgot my trip down memory lane when I noticed the thoroughly loved *Jurassic Park* VHS staring at me. It beckoned me forward to love it again. It was resting halfway down the stack of movies. Why it wasn't on the very top was a mystery, but I pulled it from its spot and held it. My fingers hovered over the cardboard box for a moment. Touching it almost felt like a sin. I suppressed my inner Christian and slid the VHS from its sarcophagus.

Along with dust and memories, two pieces of paper fluttered to the ground and perched at my feet. I picked up the first page that was a map of Wyoming with several different red X's across the state in what seemed like no pattern.

The second was folded a couple of times, demanding attention before it could be revealed. After my careful and precise unfolding, I saw that on the inside was a letter in chicken scratch handwriting, stained with Dorito powder. I rubbed my fingers over the writing which I immediately recognized as Larry's. If I left my fingers there long enough, I might have been able to feel Larry through the words. I took a deep breath and began reading the letter.

L,

I know what you're thinking: How shitty of me to leave you a letter after everything I've put you through over the years.

What did Larry mean by "everything I've put you through?" Could it possibly be that Larry knew he wasn't going to live long, and he felt guilty about leaving me behind? Or maybe he was referring to watching the same movie over and over. But that was impossible; I loved that as much as he did. He was right about one thing though—only finding a letter down there was a little shitty. I kept reading the letter anyway.

But listen,

I'm sure you're feeling antsy and are itching for adventure, so I leave you with this:

Larry was right. I had been itching for adventure! School was boring. My social life was boring. Life was boring. An adventure would really make the rest of this dreadful winter a lot more interesting.

How was it possible that, even after death, Larry knew exactly what I needed? Damn, I needed to stop getting distracted. Focus brain. Keep reading.

you know historically that dinosaurs roamed through Montana and Wyoming. Their bones remain here. Particularly, the bones of a T-Rex. A full T-Rex.

Woah. Was I reading that right?

You read that right.

Damn. I needed to just read the rest of it, so I didn't get ahead of myself again.

A full T-Rex skeleton in Wyoming. I want you to find it.

Document it. Relish in the glory. You have the map. You have the mind to solve this.

The first clue: GO FOR GOLD. Good luck. You got this.

-D

I stared at the map that had fluttered to my feet. The letter in my hand burned, signaling its desire for my attention. What could have D possibly meant? Dinosaurs? Danger ahead? No, no. It was much simpler than that. D for Dad. Larry hadn't left me with nothing. He left me with an adventure, an adventure that had everything to do with what we loved together.

I needed to tell Allen about it. There is no way that he wasn't going to be interested in what I found. He loved Friday *Jurassic Park* time just as much as me. One word in the letter kept coming back to me: *historically*. Historically. History. History!

We could use this as our project! Dinosaurs may not be a part of human history, but they were a part of the history leading up to the existence of humans. Plus, Metters wouldn't mind as long as we did our part— research and a banging presentation that would have all our classmates cheering in the auditorium.

The first thing I needed to do was go to see Allen, to get him in on the project idea. There was no way Ellison or Becky were going to have a better idea. I mean, this was dinosaurs, for fuck sake! I stuffed the letter and map into my pocket and ran upstairs.

He didn't leave me without anything, I thought, before opening the door.

A PLAUSIBLE ARGUMENT:
FOR HISTORICAL PURPOSES

The shock on Karen's face when I emerged like a hibernating bear from the basement was truly magical. It took her a moment to find her voice.

"Lyle?"

"Karen."

"It's mom. What were you doing in the basement?"

"Sorry, Karen, but I simply cannot indulge with you in casual chat right now as I need to go see my BFFL and talk to him about our history project." I began to run out the door before adding, "By the way, the basement is mad dusty, you might want to go down there and clean up before your asthma starts acting up again. And I think the pair of underwear downstairs is going to grow legs and walk up here and demand food. If that happens you better make it pay rent." I didn't turn around to see Karen's reaction, but I bet it was comical.

I ran the five blocks to Allen's house quickly. I let myself in like I always do. Allen's parents were sitting mindlessly on the couch watching reruns of Family Feud. They didn't even hear me come into the house. I just went right upstairs to bombard Allen with my mouth watering discovery.

I ran past Allen's sister's room. Juniper was having a tea party with a bunch of her stuffed animals. From what

I could see, she had invited a stuffed spider, mole, snake, and polar bear. She had a thing for scary animals and insects. Allen told me once that she asked their parents for a pet tarantula and his mother almost had a heart attack. Another time she put a plastic beetle in my jacket. I found it hours later and almost died. I tried to avoid her as much as possible. The last thing I needed was a plastic scorpion in my pants.

Juniper clanged a tea cup with her stuffed snake, and I snuck by before she saw me. She whispered something about putting venom into his tea for flavor, and I had to pick up the pace.

I found Allen almost comatose on his bed. He wasn't asleep, but his eyes were almost closed, and he was whispering sweet nothings to his ceiling. I grabbed a glass of water on his bedside table and tossed it over his face. He didn't move.

"Allen, the ceiling doesn't want to sleep with you."

"No—no. But Becky does."

"What are you even talking about you weirdo?"

"Bro," Allen sat up slowly. He reminded me of a sloth moving on a branch. Something seemed off about him today, but I couldn't figure him out. "Becky kissed me last night after I threw grass at her and she fed me brownies."

"Brownies? Allen, are you high?" I said with a laugh.

"Baked like a can of beans, baby. I ate one more this morning, just for good measure." He slid off the edge of his bed and onto the floor. "My parents are going to kill me when they emerge from their game show coma downstairs. Well, that's if they even notice." Allen smiled at me with all his teeth. He still had residue of brownie stuck in the middle of his front two chompers.

"Dude, how many brownies did you eat last night?" I asked, lowering myself down to crouch in front of Allen and look him in the eyes. They were bloodshot and glazed like a donut.

Looking him in the eyes right then was a challenge though. His eyes were darting in every direction, almost like he could see things in the room that I couldn't.

"Lyle, do you see that!" Allen pointed to an empty spot on his wall. I rolled my eyes and looked at him again.

"Bro, there's nothing there. Stop being weird," I said, but Allen's eyes grew wide and he pulled the blanket down from his bed and screamed. "Allen! Stop screaming or June is gonna come in with her creepy stuffed animals. Or worse, your parents will hear you!" I tried to yell over Allen, but he continued to scream over me.

"The meteor is coming back for us!" Allen yelled.

"How many times do we need to have the argument, Allen? Your damn space rock killed my dinosaurs and that's the end of that!" High or not, Allen knew how heated I got when he brought up the meteor that made the dinosaurs go extinct. Allen peeked his eyes out of the blanket that was covering his face.

"The meteor—it's coming back, Lyle. No shit this is real. I can see it!"

"Allen, you are tripping. There is no meteor in your room and no meteor is coming to get you, or us. And if you make one more meteor comment right now, I am going to give you the biggest wet willy of your life." Allen covered his ears and screamed again.

"Not my precious ear holes!"

"I'm gonna kill you!" I said as Allen finally pulled the blanket off him forcing him to look at me. Good, I had his attention. "You'll never believe what I found in my basement." Allen's tired eyes adjusted to stare at me more clearly. "I found a treasure map that leads to a full T-Rex skeleton in Wyoming! We have to do this for our project." I nearly screamed at him. I guess all of Allen's screaming had encouraged me to be loud.

"Can we go back to the fact that you actually went down into your basement."

"Allen, did you even hear what I just said about the T-Rex?" I stared at him with my best version of the stink eye. Allen slapped his mouth together loudly. He made a slurping noise that was both gross and uncalled for.

"Lyle, my tongue doors are numb," Allen said picking at his teeth.

"Tongue doors? Jesus Christ, Allen. Your lips?!" I yanked the blanket away from him so that he started to stroke like a cat or another small animal. This kid was truly unbelievable. He must have eaten three brownies to be this out of it, instead of the one he said he ate. But what do I know? I've never eaten one myself. "Forget the project for now, I have to go to the store to get a journal anyway. I'll see you in school on Monday and we can discuss it in history class. I'll fist fight any of you fuckers who don't want to do it." I started to leave Allen's room and looked back to see him whispering to the ceiling again. I felt guilty about leaving him alone during this time, but he was being unresponsive. "Drink a lot of water and stay away from brownies," I said before leaving.

Although seeing Allen high was probably the funniest thing I had ever seen in my young life, I couldn't help but be a little mad at him for not being as excited as I was about the T-Rex. I blamed the pot. It really did eat your brain. Oh well, I had to pester Karen for a run to the store for my journal anyway. I ran past June's room in case she tried to get me to join her macabre tea party, and I left Allen's house still without alerting his parents.

* * *

When Monday rolled around, I realized that I had spent the rest of my weekend pouring over the first clue, GO FOR GOLD, and ignoring the journal that Karen brought me. Mainly because the store only had one with unicorns on it, but also because I hadn't wanted to write anything down. I couldn't think of anything for the clue either. But I was excited to talk to Allen about this again. When I finally saw him in the parking lot, he was looking rather dapper. He might've even brushed his hair.

"Sorry about Saturday, Lyle. I was so high I thought I was on a journey through outer space. I also couldn't stop thinking about Becky kissing me. It got pretty depressing when I remembered she told me not to tell anyone though," Allen said as I met up with him in our usual spot in the parking lot.

"So, Becky did kiss you, huh?" Well, I'll be damned."

"Yeah man, you know what it was like trying to conceal a boner in jeans? Capital W for 'Wreckless.'"

"I'm gonna stop you right there because reckless starts with an 'R' not a 'W.'" Allen looked at me with sheer wonderment.

"You're joking."

"Serious as a heart attack, my friend," I said.

"My life is a lie... but anyway, about this full T-Rex skeleton I so rudely ignored, you for realsies about that?

Like, can we hunt for it like that guy from travel channel who can continuously pull off khakis with huge pockets?" Allen asked while stuffing a stick of gum into his mouth.

"Josh Gates? Hell yeah, Al. I'm telling you we can be real live versions of Josh Gates." Allen gave me a huge smile that only made me more excited about my discovery.

"Well you know how I feel about the Travel Channel. I would love to explore around. We gotta tell Becky. Oh, and Ellison. In class obviously because it'll be 'social suicide' if I talk to her out of the classroom." I buried every sarcastic comment I could think of in that moment because my excitement was taking over. I was so excited that I walked down the hallway without many visions or daydreams. Just the usual suspects, a few raptors here, a few triceratopses here, but nothing out of the ordinary. And, then, my daydreams were in good company, because I would actually be putting my knowledge to use about dinosaurs for an actual history project.

Metters started class by continuing his lecture from Friday, which I had already forgotten about and still didn't care about. I just wanted him to let us work in our project groups. Plus, I'd learned so much about WWII by that point I was actually convinced that I had stormed the beaches on D-Day. I'd never hunted a T-Rex skeleton though.

Metters had successfully sweated through his button down before he finally let us get into our groups. I've never been more excited to socialize in my life. *Dr. Calian would be proud*, I thought.

I held the confidence that neither sweaty Becky nor smarty pants Ellison would have an idea better than mine, but just to be sure I'd have to be more assertive than ever.

When I finally got together with everyone, my butt hadn't even made full contact with the chair before I started talking.

"I have our project." Full contact with the seat. Eye contact was all on me. No interruptions. "I already spoke to Allen about it and he agrees. So, you guys can't even argue with us." *Or I'd fight you.* Still no resistance. It was going much better than I expected. Maybe I'd been overlooking this whole "socializing" thing my entire life.

"Well, Lyle, what's your idea then?" Ellison was genuinely curious, an emotion I hadn't seen from him since we were little. Probably because he was a nerd and into all that education shit. Becky was too busy filing her nails to speak. Who even brings a nail file to school? That was so random. "Lyle?" Right. I was about to propose easily the greatest project of all time. I leaned in. I had to get their undivided attention.

"Long story short: I found a letter and a map documenting the historical and archaeological possibility of a full T-Rex skeleton existing, here, in Wyoming. Here's the map," I slid the map onto the table like a confidential file: for authorized eyes only. "And here's the letter with the first clue: GO FOR GOLD."

"Hold up." Record scratch. Smooth sailing aborted. The fourth party had intervened. "How do we know this is legit?"

"It's legit." Second party, Allen, to my aid. He gave Becky a tender glance. One almost too controversial for the classroom. Surely someone else noticed.

"Okayyy, but what if it's not legit and we just waste our time? I still gotta apply to college and junk and running around all of Wyoming is the last thing I want to be doing. I want to get out of here, not explore more of it." Becky clicked her tongue at the end of her statement. I wanted to fly across this table and slap her. But, one, I didn't hit girls (or anyone), and two, I didn't want Allen to be mad at me. Ellison stepped in before things got nasty.

"I'm slightly with Becky on this one guys. Why can't we just do our project on Devils Tower and the historical and spiritual impact that it has had on Native Americans for decades? This way it's right here and we don't have to go digging for clues," Ellison said, siding with Becky. Maybe it was going to be a little bit more difficult than I originally thought. Leave it to smarty pants Ellison to have another idea already. He probably thought that a project like that would look better to Princeton. I had to attack this from a different angle. I couldn't let Larry down.

"Okay, that's a good straight forward idea, but hear me out. This is the last project that we are all ever going to do in our high school careers. Why should we settle for the easy project? Why not go big? Why not show Princeton, or whatever college that you want to go to, Becky, that we are willing to get our hands dirty for our research?" I argued, hoping that I was being convincing enough to reel in the last two members of our group.

"That is the exact reason why we should just go for the easy project," Becky said. Damn she really wanted to get under my skin. How hard was it going to be to get her on board? Did she want me to get on my hands and knees and beg to her perfectly filed toenails? No way. That was never going to happen.

"Wait a minute here. You do have a point, Lyle. It would look better on college applications. Colleges love when they see that you are involved in your community. I already got into Princeton, but this can definitely benefit you, Becky." Ellison shifted to lean forward and look Becky right in the eyes. "I am willing to scrub my Devils Tower idea. But, do you have a better idea, Becky?" Ellison said, which led to a prolonged awkward period of silence from Becky. We had her. "Plus, even if it's not real Metters said that we can do the project as a county myth. I'm in, guys."

Three against one. There was no way that Becky could say no. We all stared at her while she looked down to regard her perfectly filed nails. I could see the steam running from her ears as she tried to come to a decision in her mind.

"Where did you even find this map and letter?" Becky asked.

"In the library," I lied. I smiled though and tried not to sweat. Thinking about spending prolonged time in the library made me nervous. I almost wanted to break out in hives. No one questioned me spending time in the library though. Which was good. In hind-sight, they probably should've known better.

"Any leads on what GO FOR GOLD means?" Becky looked up with the realest smile I'd ever seen on her face. Four. All in. Let's go!

"Well, I have been thinking about it all weekend, but I have to be honest, I'm not quite sure what that can possibly mean yet," I said, taking a look at the map. "The X's are all scattered across. They seemingly have no pattern to them—which means that the clue is all in the letter.

But I think we should focus on what GOLD means. Especially in Wyoming." I was trying extra hard to sound smart, so they didn't see through my façade.

"Well let's use the laptops and do some quick research with the time we have left in class," Ellison suggested. We split up to do individual research. I was struggling to even decide where to begin searching. The gold rush? Gold medals? The Olympics? None of that even made any sense. There had to be a more logical explanation for the clue—something that was connected to Larry in some way. But where? And what could it possibly be?

Instead of actually looking for an answer I just googled different dinosaurs and looked at the pictures. If I wasn't sure what the clue meant, at the very least I could get pumped up about the project.

A lightbulb went off in my head.

What if the clue wasn't gold at all? What if the clue was more metaphorical than an actual piece of gold? There were so many different possibilities at that point I thought the lightbulb inside my head might eat itself.

RESEARCH IS ONLY
BEARABLE with SWEETS

"Well if you guys have no idea what the clue means I'm not going to stick around here and wait for you to figure it out," was the last thing Becky said before grabbing her purse and leaving when the bell went off. Out of the corner of my eye, I saw Allen's face drop when Becky left seemingly uninterested. How she could go from sneaking kisses with him to wanting nothing to do with him was beyond me.

"Maybe we can go to the library and do some research on Yellowstone. You know? See if they have anything about dinosaur bones being found there before." Ellison's suggestion was a good one indeed. But that would mean staying after school later than I wanted to.

"I can't. I gotta go home right after school because I'm grounded." Oh, shit, Allen's parents must've actually found him in his comatose state. Damn. Ellison looked at me with doe eyes, almost pleading to me with his corneas to engage with him in his after-school nerd activity. Well, Dr. Calian had told me that I should hang out with people besides Allen. Plus, I used to hang out with Ellison all the time. Maybe things would be just like they used to be. Well, as long as Derek didn't show up.

"What do you say, Lyle?" As much as staying in school made my skin want to break out in anti-learning hives, I needed to figure out the mystery, and who better to help than master nerd himself?

"Okay fine, but can we grab some Slurpees beforehand? I need cherry fuel for my reading or else I won't function."

"Sounds good to me. I could go for a vanilla latte myself after school. I'll meet you out front after the final bell. See ya, Lyle." God, could he have been any more of a nerd? Either way, Ellison was my best bet then, being as Allen was side-lined for his affair with Mary Jane and Becky was more interested in being passive-aggressive about wanting to work on the project.

Allen leaned in extra close to almost shove his tongue in my ear.

"You gonna be alright with just Ellison later?" I nodded. Good ol' Al always looking out for me. "Okay good. Your afternoon is going to be much better than mine. My parents are probably going to tape my eyes open and force me to watch game shows. Talk about capital B for Boring." I laughed, but I was too busy looking at the hallway that just turned into a Jurassic jungle.

* * *

When ~~school~~ torture finally ended, I found Ellison eagerly waiting for me. It was weird seeing him not following Derek around. I was starting to feel super positive about our chances of finding info about the T-Rex skeleton. But first Slurpees.

"Are you ready to go get some research fuel?" If I stayed with Ellison alone for more than an hour I was going to start wearing button ups and Oxfords. His nerd was going to bleed into me. Like a zombie virus. Only worse. I would try to keep the talking to a minimum while we walked over to The Mart to grab our drinks. The walk started to feel awkward though. I needed something to fill the silence. A deep sexual moan. A fart. Anything.

The trees were starting to turn bionic when Ellison decided to speak. "How's your mom doing anyway?"

"What? Oh, Karen? She's great, doing her mom stuff and all." "You call her Karen now?"

"Well yeah, duh, that's her name." What a weird question to be asking me.

"I know, but you used to call her Mommy all the time when I was there." He gave me a side eye that said: *Open up to me, I know you want to.*

"Well, times have changed. You used to come over all the time too." "Yeah, about that—"

"Oh, look! The Slurpees are calling me. I might even get a Danish. I'm feeling adventurous." I sped away from Ellison to avoid a heart-to-heart in which we would reveal all of our secrets. Plus, I really had wanted a cherry Slurpee. How else was I supposed to research dinosaur bones? I watched as the red colored ice poured into my cup. The slush folded on itself in a way that I imagine the waves would swallow the sea. I had never seen the ocean, so as far as I knew it was peaceful.

I could see Ellison at the coffee machine as my Slurpee came to a perfect halt and mound underneath the plastic lid. How Ellison was going to drink hot bean juice over a delicious Slurpee was beyond me. Probably because he was a nerd.

I was just about to sneak a cheese Danish when Ellison snuck up on me.

"You ready to head out?" I wanted to slap him for the jump scare but resisted the urge. "I'll pay for your Slurpee, and the Danish you're still dangling your hand over." Now he was making me feel bad for thinking about slapping him. "But only if you grab the strawberry Danish next to yours, seems fair, yeah?"

"You had me at 'I'll pay,' plus I think I only have like, three dollars with me anyway." "Jeeze, Lyle, did you know that I was going to treat you to some snacks or something?"

"No, I was just going to smile at Jerry, the cashier, until I made him uncomfortable enough that he would just let me take them."

"Are you sure that you're not still eight?"

"Well, Ellison, we're not all bound to go to Princeton." I wiggled my eyebrows at him for effect, strengthening my continuous comedic act. "You excited to move out to the east coast?"

"It is definitely going to be an adjustment from here, but I am looking forward to all the academics. What about you, did you apply anywhere?" That conversation was starting to get too serious for me. I was still trying to avoid adulting as much as possible. I started moving toward Jerry so Ellison could pay for our goodies. I decided to humor him a little.

"Dr. Calian gave me a list of schools for creative writing, but I haven't got a chance to look at them yet. Plus, I don't write, like, at all, and I never really considered college as an option anyway."

"I think you should give it a shot. You always had a huge imagination when we were kids. There's got to be a way for you to translate that into stories." Little did he know Jerry was actually a velociraptor as he was ringing us up. His long fangs peeked outside of his top lip with a little bit of blood smeared across them from his lunch. Jerry's eyes met mine in a moment of realization—we have had this same exact staredown before. Jerry licked his fangs. One day, Jerry would try to jump across this counter and eat me—grab at me with his little velociraptor claws and shovel my innards into his mouth before the other customers noticed he was a dinosaur.

I'd been seeing a lot of velociraptors lately. I'd have to write that down to tell Dr. Calian. Maybe he would have wisdom to shed on the topic.

"You sound like Dr. Calian. Are you sure you aren't fifty?" I nudged him with my elbow to get a laugh from him, but he just stared at me with dead-pan eyes as we left The Mart.

"Lyle, you're talented and smart. You need to start taking yourself more seriously." Great. I was being scolded by Mr. Princeton.

"Alright, alright. I was only joking. Plus, we're about to be super serious and dive into research, aren't we?"

"I'm just making sure. This is the last big project of my high school career. It's important to me that we are successful." He didn't even know what the project meant to me. He would understand though, having known Larry and all. I decided to keep my true intentions to myself though. Something inside me wanted to trust him in that moment, but I just couldn't.

"Trust me," Ellison tried to cut me off, but I asserted myself over him. "I know, I know, but trust me. This project is important to me too." Ellison nodded in my direction as we continued to walk back to the library.

The wind was whipping around us in small tornados. The birds were shrieking in delight.

The sun winked at us as we entered the library. It was safe to say that the universe was egging us on. It wanted us to find this T-Rex. I was sure of it.

* * *

Ellison and I pored over our research for an hour and seven minutes (which was seven minutes longer than I actually wanted to be there) and all I found was that a sand dollar is actually a fossil called a periarchus. And I finished my Slurpee and Danish which was making me extra cranky. The periarchus would have been interesting on any other day, but I needed to find things out about dinosaur bones. I was just about to rip the book I was holding in half when Ellison started speed walking toward me with a rather large book in his hands. He looked like a mom walking up to a naughty child ready to scold it. It was a little intimidating. He slammed the book down onto the desk which caused me to lean back in shock.

"I found something that may be vital to our research." He began to flip through the book quickly.

"I can see that." I resisted making fun of him for being a super nerd. He was taking it seriously, and that meant a lot to me.

"Okay, so." The library book started to turn into a flesh-eating monster, saliva running down the course of its spine and sharp fangs ready to bite at any minute. Ellison snapped his fingers at me. "Now's not the time for daydreams, Lyle! I found what the first clue means!" Now he had my attention. I was fully listening to him. He pointed his finger at a T-Rex skeleton in the book before diving into his discoveries.

"So, it turns out that the Tyrannosaurus Rex actually lived in the Cretaceous period, not the Jurassic period. The Cretaceous period was around 70 million years ago and it marked the end of the Mesozoic era with the second largest mass extinction that planet Earth has ever been a part of."

"Wait, how is this helpful? We learned all about this in second grade science class." I was starting to get a little impatient with his explanation.

"Hold on, Lyle, I'm getting there." *Quicker would be nice.* "The Cretaceous period is the closest period to us from the Mesozoic era, meaning finding fossils from that period is much more plausible. Now, on top of that, during this time period The Rocky Mountains were rising. In basic terms, severe compressional forces operated through Idaho, Wyoming, and Utah, causing great sheets of rock to be moved and folded horizontally. Meaning, The Rockies became a resting place for bones. A perfect tomb, if you will. But that's not all." Ellison flipped further into the book. He was truly invested in this project. Probably for the good grade and guarantee of his Princeton success.

I wondered what he would do if he knew that Larry was involved in all of this. Larry was probably disappointed in me for taking so long to find the letter. But all that mattered right now was we had it and were working on finding out what this clue meant. What if that would change his perspective, knowing this was actually about Larry? Ellison seemed childish in this moment. Eight. Playing in my backyard. Laughing with Larry. Wearing a baby blue tuxedo to his funeral. Ellison told my mom he thought Larry wouldn't want him to wear black.

Why did I remember that memory in that moment?

Why?

I pulled myself from my thoughts just in time to listen to Ellison continue his explanation and watch as Derek walked into the library. One: I was surprised he even knew this section of the school existed. Two: I didn't want him to see us. I folded into myself and listened to Ellison.

"In 1990, a ninety percent recovered T-Rex skeleton was found by Sue Hendrickson in South Dakota. They named the T-Rex Sue after her."

"Woah, Sue is a pretty wimpy name for a T-Rex." I watched as Derek turned the corner out of my view.

"You're missing the point, Lyle. Sue was found in South Dakota. The Rockies folded in Wyoming, by Yellowstone National Park. The first clue must be Yellowstone. Gold may not be yellow, but it is in the family. And 'go' means the journey. Yellowstone is the first clue, Lyle!"

Ellison's excitement seeped into me and I stood to regard the book. We had already considered Yellowstone as a possibility, but the scientific evidence there didn't lie.

"How am I going to convince Karen to let us travel to the other side of the state?" Ellison started to laugh when a deep throaty chuckle engulfed Ellison's. I knew it was coming from behind me. I knew Derek found us. I turned around to find that my suspicions were correct.

"Well, well, well, what do we have here? Ellison hanging out with Lyle Farter." He seriously needed to come up with something better than farter. Even he was too grown for such an elementary insult.

"What's going on, Derek?" Ellison was too nice to him. Where Ellison spoke to him with a voice full of honey all I could think about was how many times he had picked on me.

"Came here to talk to Coach about my football scholarship to Alabama. Looks like I'm going to get a full ride just like my dad and I expected." In what world did someone like Derek get a full ride and someone like Allen would have to work two summer jobs just to attempt to go to college? "Why are you wasting your time with Farter? You stay here any longer and he will probably eat you, I know his dad would."

"We are working on a class project together, Derek. And come on man, really? Larry never did anything to you." I was actually surprised to see Ellison standing up for me. Derek scoffed at him before dramatically cracking his knuckles.

"Yes, he did. He ate all my food at the school fair." Derek's laughter filled the library. I could imagine the librarian's face as the noise continued to crack the silence. I was just about to stand up to Derek when a group of girls walked by whispering and laughing at him.

"Look, there's Derek, did you hear he shit all over Becky's bathroom?" one giggled.

"Yeah, so much for being a superstar football player if you can't even hold your bowels." Their laughter silenced Derek's as he turned to me again.

"Almost forgot, Farter, I left you a present in your locker. Let's go, Ellison I want you to be there when I tell my dad the news." In a perfect world Ellison would tell Derek to go blow and we would be BFFs again. We would start a campaign against Derek's bullying, and he would lose his scholarship to Alabama. He would spend the rest of his life following up every question with "Would you like fries with that?" But it wasn't a perfect world.

"We can talk more about the project in class tomorrow, Lyle. See ya then." I watched the two of them leave together. I picked up my Slurpee and tossed it in the trash on the way to my locker. The way I chucked it was a little overtly aggressive though, and it ricocheted off the trash can. I went over to pick it up before the librarians yelled at me for being destructive on school property.

I could already tell that Derek stuffed my locker full of something before I even opened it. It was oozing out the sides. When I opened it, cottage cheese poured all onto my jeans and the floor. Great. It was going to take another hour just to clean up. Where had he even gotten this much cottage cheese from? This was ridiculous. How come it always had to happen to me?

I found a janitor's mop and a bunch of paper towels and went to work. I swirled it back and forth.

"What are you doing?" a voice behind me asked as I stopped cleaning. I turned around to see Becky staring at me. She was wearing her class president shirt. She must have just come from a meeting.

"Cleaning up a mess that Derek left me," I said, trying to ignore her at the same time for being mean to me earlier about the project.

"Someone seriously needs to stop letting that kid get away with everything." Becky came over and picked up the paper towels and began wiping.

"Why are you helping me?"

"I feel bad for being so snappy with you earlier about not wanting to work on the project. And I am the class president, I can't just sit around and watch a student who needs help. It would be bad for my reputation," Becky explained while covering her nose to wipe up the cottage cheese. If she thinks that smelt, I could only imagine how she felt finding her bathroom covered in poop. Best not bring that up here. I did, however, see what Allen meant about her being overly cautious about her reputation. It was almost irritating how hard she tried to be perfect.

"That should be good enough, right?" I asked, looking at my finally clean locker.

"Yeah." I stared at her not sure what to say. I could have called her out about Allen, but I was feeling too defeated already. "Well, I'll see you in class," Becky said before leaving. I stared down the empty halls that were usually bustling with children, pre-teens, and full-blown young adults, to see that it lay dormant. That was why I avoided school after hours. It was creepy, and anything goes in an empty hallway. I was sure a velociraptor was lurking around the corner. I had to get out of there.

I went to my car and thought about how pissed I was at Ellison for leaving me, though he did figure out the first clue. *Yellowstone.* Now, how to get there? I drove back home while thinking of different ways to convince Karen. All of them ended in her saying no. Time to pull out the big guns, puppy dog eyes, and make a Power-Point. There was no way I wasn't going to Yellowstone.

JUST CALL ME
LITTLE TREE

If finding out what GO FOR GOLD meant was looking for the new Messiah, then convincing Karen to let me go to Yellowstone with Allen, a friend I hadn't spoken to since I was eating boogers, and a lotion-obsessed young woman, was going to be like finding the Ark of the Covenant. That's right. I pay attention in history class sometimes. It was going to be impossible. I did go as far as making a Power-Point, but I thought it was pretty stupid, so I scrapped it. The best part about it was a dog that was begging. It was cute, but not good enough to convince Karen to let me drive across the state.

Since Allen was still grounded due to his war with drugs, I didn't have anyone to hang out with after school. This meant that I was lingering around my house. Pacing and sweating. Reading the letter from Larry over and over again. Doing some research on Yellowstone. If that place was gonna blow, we better get the hell outta Wyoming.

Maybe if I show Karen the letter, she would understand why I wanted to go to Yellowstone? No, no, that would just make her try to stop me from going even more. Once she knew Larry was involved, she was going to put on her Mom brakes and call Dr. Calian for extra visits. That was how she always dealt with Larry's death—by making me talk to Dr. Calian about it instead of her.

Maybe if I explained to Karen that it was simply for

educational purposes she would understand? No, no, she's going to start asking a lot of questions about when I started to care about school projects and why this project involved driving across the state. That would lead us back to the first scenario, where she finds out it was all about Larry and then BOOM more Dr. Calian. More grief counselors.

Okay. Okay. What if I told her that it was Ellison's idea? Yes. Ellison. Use the smart one as bait here. If I told Karen that it was Ellison's idea to explore through Yellowstone, she would be more inclined to believe that. All I had to do was convince Ellison to come over and explain to Karen that it would help with his pre-Princeton career if he engaged in a hands-on project.

I would bring Allen too. This way Karen knew that Allen would be with me the whole time. Maybe I'd even ask Becky. Having a girl involved would make it seem like I was really trying to hang out with people—since I'd never brought a girl around. Karen didn't have to know that Allen had a crush on her. I could fake a little eyelash batting and kissy faces at Becky. She would probably think that it was just me being weird and I wouldn't have to worry about her getting mad.

Yes. Yes. It was all coming together nicely. And it would still keep everyone in the dark about Larry. Well, except Allen, he was always the exception. I would tell everyone in class when we talked about our project again. Larry would be proud. Me taking initiative. He would also say I deserved an award for all of my hard work. A bag of sour cream and onion chips it was.

* * *

Since Metters was obsessed with WWII, he had spent the rest of the week talking about Iwo Jima. I wanted to stab my ears with my pen, so I didn't have to listen to him mispronounce Japanese names again. Even the trees outside were tired of hearing about this. They started attacking each other with their bionic limbs.

It was starting to get juicy. This one tree (that was much smaller than the other ones) was using its stature to its advantage. It was like an ankle biting dog, going for the low limbs to take out the enemy. It was Little Tree against the Big Tree. Big Tree cracked its knuckles. Big Tree said in a shitty English dubbed voice, "You have come this far young one. Now it's time to go home."

Little Tree spat near Big Tree's feet. "Leave? Leave?" I laughed out loud at the pun. "I ain't going anywhere, Johnny. You die here." Oh, so Big Tree's name was Johnny. Interesting. I wrote that down. Just as Little Tree was charging to kill Big Tree, Metters' nasally voice cut into my daydream.

"Lyle Farker, are you going to get with your project group or am I going to have to dock points from you already?" I could feel the laser eyes Ellison was giving me for jeopardizing our project.

"Sorry, Metters. I was actually thinking about how I want to present the research that I found with my group. It takes me a little longer to gather my thoughts together. I hope you understand." I gave him a toothy grin as he ushered with his hands for me to join my group. I went over and sat down to two people giving me the stink eye and Allen smiling.

"Well, Ellison, did you tell them what we found out?" Ellison rolled his eyes at me and scoffed. He was mad. I had to find a way to make him less mad. That way I could convince him to come to my house after school. But it wasn't Ellison who answered.

"Yes, he told us. And I always knew you were weird Lyle, but now I know you are just crazy. There is no way in hell you are going to get me to Yellowstone. I'm over this project." Becky slumped into her chair. I wished I could ask Allen to give her kisses and convince her, but I knew that was too risky. I had to think of another way to get her on board.

That was when I saw it. The sand dollar necklace that hung from her neck.

"See that necklace you're wearing?" I pointed to it as she took it into her hands. "Do you know what that is?"

"I'm not an idiot, Lyle. It's a sand dollar." I had her then.

"Yes, Becky, but do you know what it is?" She stared at me blankly. Allen was looking at me with interest now too.

"It's called a periarchus. It's a fossil that washes up on the beach. It existed around the same time as dinosaurs did. It's actually really rare. We could find some of those along the way too." Becky twirled her necklace back and forth between her fingers.

"I've always wanted to go to the beach," she mumbled. Allen took the opportunity to place a tender hand on her shoulder. Ellison and I exchanged a knowing glance.

"Becky, I know you hate it here, but that's here. In this small town that we have all been stuck in since we were born. Yellowstone would be traveling. Sure, it's in the same state, but it's still away from here." Allen rubbed Becky's shoulders in small even circles. She sighed.

"But my friends—"

"If that's what you're worried about, then just tell them it's for a project." The lightness in Allen's voice tightened when she mentioned her superior social status. One step forward. Three steps back.

"Okay, but how are we even going to get there?" It was my time to shine.

"About that—I have a plan. Can you guys all come to my house after school today, so we can talk to Karen? It should only take about a half an hour, so you won't have to worry about it cutting into your Friday too much. I think that if we all talk to Karen together, she will understand and let us borrow the car for the weekend."

"Of course, I love Karen." Allen—ready player two.

"It's been so long since I've seen her. Too long." I'd take that as a yes, Ellison. Ready player three. And of course, as always, we were waiting on Becky. I batted my eyelashes at her for practice. She made a weird face and shuffled uncomfortably.

"I mean—whatever, sure. Not sure why you call your mom by her first name though, you weirdo."

"Perfect. She gets off of work at 5. So, let's all plan to meet at my house at 6. She loves company, so she will probably try to feed all you guys too. So, come hungry." I smiled at all of them. Mostly because again I knew Larry would be proud. I was in such a good mood that I ignored Becky's comment about me being weird. And also, because Little Tree defeated Johnny outside the window and was carrying his head away in victory. Shit that was dark. Little Tree was a savage. I'd tell Dr. Calian about that.

The bell rang and we left class. Allen was walking with me to our next period.

"This is shaping up to actually be pretty successful, huh?" There was a sadness in his voice that I hadn't heard before.

"Al, you okay?" When he looked at me, I could tell he wasn't. His eyes were bloodshot, holding back tears to avoid being made fun of by younger students in the school.

"She's never going to let me be with her, is she?" I placed an arm around his shoulder and pulled him close to me.

"Hey, Al, she's just one girl. I know it doesn't seem that way, but she's just one girl." Allen's head hung and swayed side to side from his sadness. He looked like a defeated dinosaur walking through the hallways. That's when I had an idea. "Hey, it's Friday."

"Yeah, still gotta see her at your house later though and that's capital F for—"

"No, no. That's not what I'm talking about. I was talking about you coming back to my house and watching *Jurassic Park* like the old days. Dust off the old couch. Pick up some Mountain Dews on the way home?" That got Allen's attention. He shot right up at the thought.

"Lyle, are you sure you want to do that?" I let go of Allen's shoulder, so I could look him straight in the eyes.

"Hell yeah I do. Plus, Larry always said you look like a pigeon when you cry, so I am trying to save you from the embarrassment." Allen punched me in the arm.

"Then I'm in. My parents finally have released me from the game show coma. It's safe to say that I am never taking brownies from a pretty girl again. Did I tell you I saw whales in the sky? It was crazy shit."

"No, Al, but that sounds like something you would see when you were high. All you think about is the stars. And you just HAD to bring up the meteor revolving around you-know-what."

"Whoops! My bad. But that's not all I think about! I am currently thinking of Mountain Dew." He had me there. We continued to walk through the hallways to our next class. That night was going to be a good night. That was, if the celestial whales had anything to say about it.

* * *

Allen and I scooped up our Mountain Dews before we went to my house. Karen was still working when we got back. It was about 2:30, so we still had prime *Jurassic Park* viewing time before Karen would roll up and start asking questions.

Allen hadn't been in my basement since we were eight, so it made sense that he was descending the stairs like he was about to see one million dollars in gold. I was taking in everything I saw not even a week ago when Allen let out a monstrous groan.

"Wow! It looks exactly the same!" He ran over to the TV and stroked it lovingly. I stayed behind on the last stair on the staircase as Allen dragged a finger across the TV. The dust gathered on his fingertips and he rubbed them together like a greedy fly. "Can't wait to break this bad boy in again. You still have the VHS?"

"Yeah, it's right there." I pointed to the spot in which *Jurassic Park* slept. The same spot where I found the letter and the map. I made sure to put it back exactly where I found it. The basement felt abandoned. A museum stuck in the 90s. That all changed when Allen put the movie into the VHS player, sunk into the black leather couch, and started slurping on his freshly cracked Mountain Dew. I continued to watch him from the bottom step as he settled in and looked at me.

"Oh, shit, Lyle. I'm so sorry. We can go back upstairs if you want." I would admit, I was starting to sweat a little. But not enough to forget the promise that I made to my friend. I released my titanium grip on the stair banister and joined Allen on the couch.

Allen was staring at the picture of me, Larry, and Uncle Danny. He pointed at it and had a huge grin on his face.

"Dude, I think I still have that Batman shirt somewhere. You know, the one that's all fake distressed? I remember stealing it from you because I was jealous that you had one and I didn't."

"Wait. You stole my Batman shirt? I blamed Karen about that for like, three weeks. Now I am going to have to apologize." I looked down to regard the T-Shirt I was wearing. It just happened to be another Batman shirt, but this one was from Old Navy. "You know what Al, I dress sexier now anyway, so all is forgiven. Let's watch this movie!" I sank in to match Allen's comfort level. "Now, no talking about Becky or school during the movie. Deal?"

"Deal! Now press play, man." It had been a decade since I'd seen this movie, but I could still quote every line. Allen could as well. We sat there together without saying a word except for the ones that fell from the actor's lips. My favorite scene was still the showdown between the T-Rex and the raptors. It always had me on the edge of my seat. Heart pumping. My pulse didn't calm down until the credits began to roll. I was still sweating, but now it was from excitement. I sniffed my armpit. It held an odor that Larry would be proud of.

"WOOO!" Allen stood excitedly to stretch. "I mean, Chris Pratt is a hunk and all, but nothing beats the original." I couldn't help but laugh. He was right after all. I started to rise from the couch and took *Jurassic Park* out of the VHS to return it to the original spot. I began to walk towards the stairs. I didn't want to overstay my welcome down there. Allen didn't say a word.

He just followed me upstairs.

I wanted to think that Allen knew I didn't want to be down there longer than needed.

Sometimes it was almost like we shared the same brain. He didn't probe me with questions about why I left so quickly. He just allowed for me to set the pace and he went along with it.

We sat down at the kitchen table like proper gentlemen. I even folded my hands.

"Do you really think Karen is going to let us take her car to go to Yellowstone?" Did I? I could only hope that she could see I was trying to be better. A better student. A better friend. A better human. I hoped that she would understand that *at least* I was trying to recover after all these years. My grief counselors all told me to move on, to visit his grave and say goodbye—ten years was too long to still be coping—I wanted to scream in their faces, tell them that everyone grieves differently.

How can you tell an eight-year-old kid to just get over it? How can you tell anyone at any age to just get over the death of someone who was always there? Someone told me that grief comes in waves, but I guess grief counselors didn't believe in that sort of thing.

"Well, Al, I guess we are just going to have to put on our big boy pants and try as hard as possible." And try I did.

With that the doorbell rang. Someone was early. But this would give us more time to prepare. It was probably Ellison. He was always eager to engage in something if it was educational. I opened my door to find Becky standing there. She put up a finger to signify not to speak to her until she was finished with her text message. If I was a raptor, I would've eaten her as a snack. I bet she's crunchy.

"Sorry, that was super important. Well, are you going to let me in?" I stared at her, baffled for a moment, before stepping aside to let her into my house. She walked only a few steps before I felt like stirring the pot.

"Your boy is in the kitchen to the right." She turned back and gave me the nastiest look. She might've even hissed. I knew it, she was a raptor.

Allen rolled his eyes at me and gave me a look that said: *Come on man, you know that's gonna piss her off.* But I didn't care. She was messing with my best friend's feelings, and in my book I simply wasn't okay with that.

We all sat together awkwardly at the table. I had never thought that I'd want to sit in Metters class more. Or have Ellison there as a buffer. Anything to save me. But the awkward silence continued until all I could think about was Larry sitting downstairs in the basement, eating snacks and watching TV. It was 2008 again, a greasy slice of pizza hung out of my mouth, and everything was alright.

TROUGH OF
THE STORM

When Karen came home, she found four well-behaved high school seniors sitting around her dinner table talking about a history project. Ellison rolled up not too long after Becky which helped with making the air less sexually tense. If Becky gave Allen bedroom eyes one more time, I was gonna leave the kitchen.

Ellison got everyone on the same page by bringing up the project just in time for Karen to walk in. The look on her face was transcendent, like a bigfoot enthusiast seeing sasquatch for the first time in the wild, documenting it, and shoving it into the faces of the non-believers. I even batted my eyelashes at Becky before introducing her to Karen. Karen gave me a smile saying: *Wow, Lyle, I didn't know that you had it in you to bring such a lovely girl here.* Little did she know the only one at the table that "had it in him" was Allen.

Just as I'd expected, Karen offered to whip up some sandwiches for everyone. We kept the conversation to a minimum while we were eating dinner. Allen and I wolfed down our food like proper gentlemen. Ellison took slow, dignified bites like a well pampered dog. Becky might as well have not even eaten because she picked apart her sandwich like a bully would do to any undeserving freshman at school. Once everyone was finished eating, I decided now would be a good time to bring up the project.

"So, Karen, we are working on a history project and we need your help." Karen gave me an interesting look like she smelt a skunk or a raunchy fart. A Bigfoot fart, specifically.

"You need my help?"

"Well, sort of. You won't have to do any of the work, we will be doing all of that. More like, we need your assistance." I looked to Ellison. I should've warned him that I was going to throw him under the bus here, but I figured this would be more practice for his time at Princeton. "Ellison, care to explain?"

Ellison choked on his water. I had to at least try to set him up there.

"The project is a hands-on one, Karen. It was Ellison's idea because it will look good for his pre-Princeton career. Right Ellison?" Ellison was still choking on his water. I looked to Becky who was staring at Allen. God damnit this woman isn't helping with our fake crushes on one another.

"Lyle is right," Allen chimed in. "But it will also help my college applications. If some of the schools I applied to see that I was engaged in a project that involved both research and fieldwork, they might be more inclined to give me a bigger scholarship which would greatly help my parents." Allen always came in with the clutch. I swore we shared the same brain sometimes the way we read each other's minds. Karen was giving all of us the stink eye. She was suspicious.

"What is the project?" Karen swirled her water around in her glass. You would think it was a glass of whiskey the way she was nursing it.

"It's a Wyoming County project. All we have to do is

pick a historical event from Wyoming and do a project on it," I said, giving her the biggest grin I could muster.

"Plus, Mr. Metters said that if we do something that involves field research, we will get extra points, which never hurt." Allen with the sly lie to amp things up.

"And Lyle has already done a bunch of research on it, see this necklace?" Becky lifted her necklace and showed Karen. "It's like a fossil and he found that out." Karen drank in the four of us like the water she wasn't sipping. We were all on edge, fidgety. It was apparent that Karen might be indulging in a four-course dessert.

"This all sounds lovely and I'm glad that you all are working so hard on it, but I still don't know why you need my help." Karen smacked her lips together and smiled. It was the most crucial part in convincing Karen to let us borrow her car. If we slipped up then there would be no turning back, and the last thing I wanted to do was let Larry down.

"For the field research part, we need to travel around Wyoming, and we were wondering if you would allow us to borrow your vehicle in order to obtain the research we need to be truly successful in our historical endeavors." No one could have articulated that statement better than Ellison himself. He even used big SAT words. Well, "endeavors" was a big word for me.

"Travel where?" Karen leaned forward interested. We got her now.

"Yellowstone, Ms. Farker." Becky inched closer to Allen when she answered. I was almost certain she was resting a hand on Allen's upper thigh at the moment. Jesus Christ, not at the dinner table you savages.

"Yellowstone National Park? Across the state?" Karen

leaned forward again. She was almost laying on top of the table at this point.

"Yes, Ms. Farker. But we would all go together." Allen was making it difficult for me to bat my eyelashes at Becky; but, I tried anyway. Finally, Karen put the glass of water to her lips and took a huge gulp. The time she was taking to swallow was painful.

"No." Karen's single word answer floated into the air and suffocated it. My heart began to beat out of my chest and up into my throat where I was beginning to choke on it. I could feel the tears begin to prick at the corner of my eyes, but I fought them.

"Karen, why not?" I challenged her in a low tone. Maybe it was a good time to tell her the truth—that this was about Larry. That I needed this.

"I am really proud of you kids for wanting to do something like this but driving across the state is implausible. It seems like the library you have at school has ample enough information for you guys to come up with a solid project. Plus, Ellison, we all know you already got into Princeton. And Allen you always find a way to make money—you've been trying to sell me half eaten slices of pizza since you were little." The more Karen talked and made sense of the situation, the angrier I got. Why did she always have to have a leash on me? I let the words spill from my mouth before I thought about them.

"No, Karen, we need to do the project this way. And we would really appreciate it if you would help us out here." My voice was shaking, and I was starting to sound like a child. The wind in the backyard began to whip up into a hurricane that I knew wasn't truly there. The bionic trees were no match for the howling that was assaulting their limbs and tearing them apart. A bolt of lightning streaked across the sky, jolting the deep gray into a moment of temporary blindness.

"Lyle, you are my son and you are going to do what I say. Have YOU even applied to college yet? Because it seems to me like all your friends here have. What does this project mean to you if all you're interested in is finishing high school?" She started to question my motives, she must have been able to read on my face that I wasn't telling her the whole truth. She always said that she knew when I was lying—knew when I was holding back from my potential. My upper lip quivered before I could stop it. How was I supposed to tell her the truth? How would she ever truly understand? The tears that once threatened to stain my face disappeared and turned into anger.

"You have no idea what you're talking about, Karen. This project means a lot to me and my friends." I thought that was what Karen wanted—for me to be dedicated to something. Anything really. Anything that wasn't hiding in my house and running away from my past. I thought Karen would at least understand that I tried. I tried to be a good student. I tried to make friends and be silly and plaster a stupid fake smile on my face when all I wanted to do was scream. Scream and scream, because whether or not Karen realized it, me getting into college wasn't going to bring Larry back.

"Since when does anything mean something to you, Lyle?" My friends began to coil towards the door as the hurricane began to rip the house from its foundation. At any moment we would be flying through the sky, maybe as far as space. Far enough for Allen to study the stars, for Becky to get out of Wyoming, for Ellison to get his PhD. I wanted to tell them to leave. To get out of here before the storm consumed them too.

I wanted to yell over the storm. To raise my voice loud enough for Karen to hear. *I DO CARE. I. DO. CARE.* But no matter how loudly I yelled in my mind, it seemed that Karen would never really hear me.

"Karen, why do you have to be like this?!" My scream echoed across the kitchen like the snap of lightning outside. The storm continued to encroach. I gave a side hand motion to Allen, who understood me.

"What did you just say to me?" I was vaguely aware of Allen ushering Becky and Ellison out my front door in the last moment before hell broke loose. I wanted to stop them from going out into the storm. I wanted to save them from the tempest that would no doubt trouble them. I wanted to save them like I wanted to save Larry. But I stood there. I stood there as the hurricane ripped the roof off of my house and the rain poured over me. I stood like a wet dog who had no home to return to—whose life was ripped up by the roots.

"You heard me," was the last thing I said before going into my room and tearing it apart.

The hurricane that once spun outside now existed inside my room. I pulled the jeans from my closet and tossed them. I wanted to tear the whole house to the ground. This was *Jurassic Park* and I was the Tyrannosaurus Rex. This place would cease to exist when I was finished with it. It would never reopen.

I let the screams rip apart my lungs into my pillow case. Karen would never understand. She never did, and she never would. I screamed and screamed until there was nothing left in my throat but shattered vocal cords.

Hours must have passed with me lying face down into my bed. The hurricane now gone, my limbs refused to rise. It was then that I felt a gentle hand rub my back. I knew it was Karen, but I refused to acknowledge her. She mumbled something about how she was sorry and that all she was trying to do was protect me. Her voice faded into the distance as I let sleep grip me.

I don't remember having any dreams that night. My sleep was plagued by the blank void I felt inside my chest, a thick metronome that clicked back and forth to mimic my failures.

THEY ROAMED
HERE, ONCE

When I woke up the next morning, I was almost embarrassed to go downstairs and face Karen. It was truly childish of me to throw a raging temper tantrum about her not allowing us to take her car across the state. We knew it was a stretch from the beginning, but something she said shook me. Karen really thought that I didn't care about anything, and somehow that was hurtful. I tried to put all of my jeans back into the closet and straighten up a little bit. Truth be told, I was stalling going downstairs.

I was worried about Becky and Ellison seeing me like that. They probably thought that I was crazy or something. Or simply an immature hot-head who couldn't control his emotions when he was told "no" about something. I texted Allen just to be safe.

> Hey Al, you think Becky and Ellison are suspect about yesterday?

Nah, I told them Karen makes you mad.

> And they bought it?

Yeah. Becky agreed right away.
Said she can't stand her parents

either. I wouldn't worry about it
too much.

Am I insane?

I erased the last text. I probably shouldn't let my buddy
know that I was currently having an existential crisis. He
had enough on his plate and had already saved my buns
once that week. I knew I needed to give him space.

When I finally grew a set of balls, I found Karen sitting
in the kitchen with Dr. Calian.

She must have called him while I was asleep. They
were drinking adult beverages like coffee and having small
talk about how Dr. Calian's daughters were doing. I was
honestly surprised to see you there. I didn't know you took
house calls.

"Ah, Lyle, you're awake." It was Dr. Calian who
greeted me with words. Karen simply sat there with a
concerned look on her face that made me want to retreat
back into my bedroom and make it spotless. "Come, sit
down; we can have a chat."

I joined them at the table hesitantly. I was used to
speaking with Dr. Calian but not with Karen in the room.

"Say, Doc, isn't it against the law for someone else to
be here during our meetings?" I was trying to be chipper,
but my voice came across as defiant and childish no doubt
because I was still angry about what Karen said the night
before.

"Usually, Lyle, yes. There are laws that protect the
confidentiality of the student, but in this case your mother
is worried that you may attempt to hurt yourself;
therefore, she may be present during this conversation."
In that moment I thought that Karen was taking things to

the extreme. That it was unnecessary. And it was really weird; I was still in my pajamas. But that was what Karen always did. When she couldn't handle me anymore, she automatically phoned the Doc.

"Have you been keeping a journal like we discussed, Lyle?"

"Yes, Doc, I actually had a lot of things that I wanted to discuss with you about that." I wanted Dr. Calian and Karen to know that I was trying. That yesterday was a fluke brought on by Karen not allowing me independence. "I have been seeing a lot of raptors lately, bionic trees fighting, and I even wrote down that I have been socializing with other people besides Allen.

Particularly an old friend, Ellison, and a new friend, Becky Road." Calling both of them my friends was a stretch, but I figured it would help my case here.

"That's good progress, Lyle. And you are in a project group with them?" Karen must have spilled all the beans before I was even able to comb my hair this morning.

"Yes, we are doing a project on Wyoming history."

"For Mr. Metters' history class, yes. I have spoken to him about it and he has stated that you have been working extra hard on the project, although you are still detached from his lectures revolving around WWII." Metters was even slightly on my side there, why couldn't Karen see that?

"To be frank, Doc, WWII is boring. I have learned about it in almost every history class I have taken. I am pretty sure the teachers in the womb even taught me about WWII. It would be more interesting if they taught us about Eastern history for once." Karen sighed as I spoke to defend myself.

"This was what I was talking about. He gets super defensive about everything instead of owning up to the fact that he isn't doing what is expected of him. I don't even think he has spent any time considering what he wants to do with his future." Karen took a sip of her coffee. I wanted to tell Karen that that wasn't true. I had spent plenty of time thinking about the future.

Her idea of success was big universities and scholarships and becoming a lawyer or some other fancy career. My idea of success was happiness.

"To be fair, Ms. Farker, Lyle is right. Our history department needs to make some changes regarding its curriculum. It is fair that a young man his age with attention span issues would be experiencing some troubles concentrating on a subject that he already knows. Mr.

Metters did mention that he isn't paying attention, but he still receives A's on all of his tests and quizzes." Dr. Calian for the win. Literally the only person there who wasn't with me was Karen. I just wanted her to believe in me. Just this once. "Lyle, have you looked into the schools I have given you regarding creative writing?"

"Nah, I haven't gotten the chance. I've been spending all my time researching for the project."

"Since your mother already made it clear that she will not be allowing you to do the field work for the project, this will give you all the time you need to apply to some schools that accept rolling submissions. It is never too late to consider college as an option, Lyle." I wanted to fight against it, but knew there was nothing that I could say to allow the conversation to sway in my favor.

"Okay." Karen looked shocked that I had folded so

easily. "But I am still going to work on this project because whether or not either of you realize it, it means a lot to me that my group is successful. This is the first time that I've cared about school since Larry was alive. I'm sorry, but I need to focus on the immediate future, not the possibility of finding a college that is right for me." It finally sounded like there was conviction in my voice. I got up from the kitchen table and excused myself. I was going to prove to Karen and Dr. Calian that I wasn't a child and I could take care of myself.

If that meant applying to schools for creative writing that I didn't even care about, fine. If that meant ignoring the juicy fights outside of classroom windows, fine. If that meant spending more time in the library, fine. Larry was never a pterodactyl circling me to make sure I did everything his way. But Karen was, and I would show her that I had what it took to be passionate about something. I didn't care about school, but I would prove to Karen and Dr. Calian that I did care about something.

* * *

I spent the next month keeping mostly to myself except for my excursions with Allen.

Even those began to thin out once he started seeing Becky in secret. He told me that they would meet up in all these different odd places like the alley behind the deli or a dimly lit parking lot of an abandoned building. I tried to tell him that that sounded more like the opening of an episode of *Snapped*, but he didn't listen to me.

I carried around my notebook and would write down every time I saw something out of the ordinary. Dr. Calian began to call them "daydreams brought about by unresolved grief" in our weekly Saturday meetings. However, without fail, each visit I would have pages upon pages filled out about what I saw. They looked something like:

- Feb. 5, 2019: Lewis and Clark exploring the hallways again—still more interesting than Metters' class.
- Feb. 5, 2019: Biconical Robot showdown in Metters' class—Little Tree defeats Johnny for the third day in a row.
- Feb. 5, 2019: Sassy mashed potatoes at lunch (first time encounter)—they wore lipstick and thick earrings—tried to give me advice about fashion by saying that wearing too many t-shirts will make me look sloppy, and I will never be taken seriously in the business world. Their mashed potato lips moved up and down in a sloppy motion like a bulldog eating peanut butter. They then said that I should be brushing my hair more often and wearing button downs (note to self: mash potatoes are fraternizing with Ellison). I honestly have no idea where this one came from, maybe from spending too much time with Becky?
- Feb. 5, 2019: Raptors crossing the street on the way home (as always).
- Feb. 5, 2019: Moon landing happened in my bedroom before bed—more interesting than expected, Neil Armstrong seems nice. Not sure why so many people think the moon landing was a hoax. The boot print on the moon is clearly from that exact space suit.

February 5, 2019, was a rather dull day, actually. It

only took two pages to explain. But as February trudged on, Ellison finalized his housing situation with Princeton, Allen and Becky were unofficially officially dating in secret, and I was able to turn in three shitty college applications to some colleges in Wyoming. I even snuck in a fourth for a college out in New York City, but didn't tell Karen about that.

Karen and I hadn't spoken much since she sat down with Dr. Calian and me. She would make sure I was doing my homework, applying to schools, and visiting Dr. Calian, but that was about it. I figured she was extra busy with work because tax return season was soon.

It was the first Sunday in March when I finally decided to pull myself out of the aftermath of Hurricane Lyle and actually go somewhere. I figured Karen would, at the very least, let me borrow her car and take it over to the stream only about fifteen minutes away. Larry used to try to teach me to fish there when I was little, but I was too interested in catching frogs and trying to put them in my mouth or throwing sticks in the water. On a good day, I would try to dive into the shallow stream head first and Larry would come running after me yelling obscenities. These were the only times I had ever seen Larry run. The only other time I was successful here was when I caught the big fish from the picture in my basement.

Just as I was about to sneak up on Karen and ask her, I was dumbfounded to find her sitting on the couch with my Uncle Danny. They were holding glasses and laughing. When Karen caught a glimpse of me out of the corner of her eye, she put on a voice that didn't quite sound like her own.

"Oh, Lyle, good you're up! Why don't you come join

your Uncle Danny and me for a chat!" She was extra exuberant which was making me suspicious. I hadn't seen my Uncle Danny since Larry's funeral. He never made it a point to stay in touch with us. He was, however, the spitting image of Larry. There was no doubt they were twin brothers. Except Uncle Danny was much thinner than Larry ever was.

I vaguely remember a conversation Larry and Uncle Danny had when I was little about a new type of exercise that was coming out and it was going to be huge. Long story short, Uncle Danny became obsessed with it, Larry didn't, and I was pretty sure that type of exercising became Crossfit. I never saw how Crossfit was exciting. It seemed like a whole lot of work. And exhausting. Who wanted to do gymnastics and dead weight lifting in one day? I was starting to get super distracted when Karen cleared her throat, bringing me back to reality.

"Actually, Karen, I was gonna ask if I could borrow the car to take it over to the old stream Larry used to take me to when I was little." Uncle Danny gave my mom a weird look, one that said: *Since when do you allow your son to call you that?* Karen thought for a moment.

"You rarely get to see your Uncle Danny, Lyle. Why not stay just for a little bit?" My mind was telling me just to sit my ass down on the couch and have a fake conversation with Uncle Danny for a little bit. He would ask me how I was doing, and I would say good. He would ask me how school was, and I would say good. He would ask me if I had a girlfriend, and I would laugh in his face. But I didn't want to sit there and force a conversation with Larry's estranged brother.

"Uhm, it's actually been ten years since I've seen

Daniel." Karen strained every vein in her face to not scream at me. She even flinched at me calling Uncle Danny by his "real adult name." Karen was about to stand up and duke it out with me, but Uncle Danny stepped in first.

"He does have a fair point Karen. I have not been around for a long time. It makes sense that he would be skeptical about my motives. Which actually leads me to why I came here in the first place. I went to visit Larry. Talk to him a bit. 'Bury the hatchet' I believe is the cliché." Now I stared at Karen. She must not have warned Uncle Danny that talking about Larry was actually a big no-no in the Farker household. "I wanted to apologize for not being more—well present after Larry's death."

"Well, no one was," I said before thinking. Shit. I really needed to start carrying around a bunch of duct tape. That way I would stop saying things I would regret. Karen didn't say anything though, and I could sense that Uncle Danny was beginning to pick up on the awkward aura in the living room.

"Well, anyway. When was the last time you guys went to the grave? It seemed very well taken care of." I take back what I said about Uncle Danny being able to read a room. He was about as perceptive as a blind veggie-saur in the middle of a T-Rex den.

"We actually don't talk about that," I said hoping that Uncle Danny would finally take the hint and stop hounding me. He was stunned into silence and just stared at me like I had five heads. Now was my chance to escape. "Is it okay if I borrow your car, Karen? I have a good idea for a short story and need to go to the old stream to see some things there. Ya know, make it accurate and all."

"Okay, Lyle, but make sure to be home before dinner."

I ran into the kitchen to snatch up the keys and slid my Chucks on at the door, all while I made sure to ignore Uncle Danny and his probing questions about Larry. When I closed the door behind me, I lingered for a moment to see if I could pick up on what they were talking about. The murmuring was low, but I strained the cochlea in my ear to hear what they were saying. I could only make out bits and pieces.

"Karen, do you think he is ever going to get over it?" Long pause. Pause was becoming uncomfortable. Pause was officially overstaying its welcome. Uncle Danny intervened. "What about you, Karen. Are you ever going to get over it?"

"I'm trying my best right now."

I peeled myself away from my front step to avoid hearing any more of the conversation. I had never considered that maybe Karen was still struggling with Larry's death as well. Maybe she was seeing raptors too? No, no, that's silly. Karen was a strong woman. A strong mother. There was no way she was still wrestling with Larry's death. Or was she just really good at hiding it, like me?

The drive over to the old stream was longer than I remembered, but I remembered how to get there perfectly. I told Karen I was there to write a short story, which was a lie. I tried the whole short story thing and it wound up being about a kid who was obsessed with dinosaurs, and I ain't trying to write a memoir, so I scrapped it.

In truth, I came to the stream to see if I saw anything new. If my imagination could conjure up something that might be worthy of a story. I sat at the edge of the stream next to the old Rocky Mountain Maple tree that was falling apart. There was a hole in it big enough to cram my entire head through. The frogs were gone this time of year, and the stream was still pretty much frozen, so no impromptu swimming for me. I let the light breeze flow into my uncombed hair (I didn't take the mashed potatoes' advice) and listened.

No birds. No cars. No new visions. Nothing. Not even a single dinosaur clouded my vision—Larry dino or regular.

GO
VIKINGS!

The following day at school, Allen and I were greeted by cameras and journalists asking us what we were doing to save the Wyoming Wildlife. Every year, our school puts together a fundraiser where everyone gets together, plays games, sells brownies (the non-medicinal kind), and someone slides down a huge blow-up slide with streamers popping off on national television.

This year was Derek's turn, and I was sure he was going to make it a spectacle.

I had completely forgotten about the fundraiser, so when I saw Allen coming in with a platter of cupcakes, I thought we were celebrating something more exciting.

"Dude, can we pretend that we both brought those cupcakes, so the principal doesn't get mad at me for not participating?" I asked Allen. He huffed at me.

"Fine, but you owe me. Finding cupcakes with bison on them wasn't easy," Allen said as we walked inside. It was what I imagined a studio of a film set looked like. People were running around frantically everywhere. Someone was dressed up in a giraffe suit, which geologically makes no sense for Wyoming, but who was I to spoil "Save the Wildlife" day? One would think having a fundraiser that created loads of trash would do the exact opposite of saving the wildlife, but I wasn't going to be the one the break the news about that.

Allen and I walked past Thadeous and Aimee who were whispering all secretive-like into Aimee's locker. They were passing something between one another. Seemed a little sketchy to be selling drugs out in the open. I didn't take either of them as the drug type, either.

Maybe I should stay away from the brownies then. As should Allen.

The only good part about the fundraiser was that we didn't have to go to any scheduled classes. We got to spend all day in the gym with screaming five-year-olds who were trying to win a stuffed sperm whale.

The gym was filled with various different booths. Some of them had pamphlets about wildlife conservation. Others were games like popping balloons or trying to toss a hacky sack through a hole. The center of the gym housed a huge blow-up slide in the shape of a white whale. I think they were trying to go for a "save the whales" motif here, but all I could think of was *Moby Dick*. All in all, the day was supposed to be fun. "Supposed to," being the key phrase.

As Allen and I meandered from stall to stall we finally came up to the student council one led by Becky. She gave us the side eye, but that didn't stop Allen from approaching her.

"Hey, Becks. Where should we put these cupcakes?" Becky winced at Allen calling her by a nickname, and the two other girls standing there giggled in an immature fashion. Becky ignored Allen completely and looked at me with daggers for eyes.

"And what did you bring to support the wildlife, Lyle?

"Allen and I made those cupcakes obviously. Now, where do they go?" Becky snatched the cupcake platter from Allen's hands.

"You boys are in luck, turns out our table actually needed a good snack!" Becky winked at Allen while the other girls were too busy checking out a news reporter wearing abnormally tight pants. This whole hot and cold routine between the two of them was making me gag. Just kiss and make-up already. Or make-out? I'm not sure what they should've done actually. "This way more people will come to our table too."

"Maybe if you picked a more interesting topic people would feel inclined to stop by." "Lyle!" Allen elbowed me in the ribs which caused me to wince.

"Ouch!" I picked up their colorful pamphlet about jellyfish and passed it to Allen. "All I'm saying is there are a lot more interesting animals out there than jellyfish. They just look like floating plastic bags."

"That's actually part of the problem, Lyle. See, you would know that if you actually read the pamphlet." Becky ripped the pamphlet from my hands and held it up. "The reason we chose jellyfish is BECAUSE they look like plastic bags. That means seals and other animals eat plastic bags by accident, thinking they are jellyfish. This causes problems in their digestive tracts, and ultimately they die from it." I took the pamphlet back from Becky.

"Interesting lecture, *Becks*. But save it for the first graders." I walked away before she was able to continue lecturing me. That day was about conservation, not about learning.

Allen and I spent the next half an hour wandering around the gym, avoiding talking to people, and dodging the unsupervised children who ran around like rabid dinos. Eventually Principal Biggs came in and announced that everyone was to find a seat in the bleachers so they could begin the live-televised portion of the day.

To my dismay, Becky found her way back to us and sat with us in the bleachers. She was still holding the pamphlets from earlier, as if to rub them in my face. I could see Ellison standing next to Derek's father, who was giving directions to the cameramen in a dramatic and aggressive fashion. I could hear him yelling about the "perfect angle" to capture Derek sliding down Moby Dick. Principal Biggs blew an air horn and the entire gym became eerily silent.

Cameras rolling in three...two... the reporter standing in front of the slide adjusted his tie and Derek perched himself on top of the slide...one...

"I am standing inside the gym of Harper K-12 in Crooks County, Wyoming as they come together to fundraise for the Wyoming Wildlife Conservation. Principal Biggs and the Harper Vikings have been doing this for ten years now, isn't that great!" Everyone around me began to cheer, but I was stuck watching Thadeous and Aimee, who were hiding in a doorway on the opposite side of the gym. What the hell were they doing? There was no way that the drugs were affecting them that badly. "We are proud to say that Harper was able to fundraise more than ten thousand dollars here today! And with that we celebrate."

The cameras tilted up to get Derek's best angle and the poppers exploded like gunshots. For a sick moment, I feared that Thadeous and Aimee were doing something much worse than trading their favorite pot gummies in the hallway. Derek began his slide down Moby Dick, and right behind him was a brown, smeared trail that followed him from the top all the way to the bottom. The gleaming white accent from Moby Dick didn't help the display of what clearly looked like Derek had shit himself (for the second time if the school had anything to say about it).

In that moment I couldn't catch my breath. My ears were ringing to the tune of the Imperial Death March. And just when my momentary deafness was lifted, the whole gym erupted into a new kind of explosive laughter. The first graders were nearly rolling on the floor. Even some teachers were laughing.

Derek, who still had no clue what had happened, was yanked away from the cameras by his father. I could see the reporter signaling for the cameras to go off air. But it was too late. That was the problem with live television. You couldn't take it back. Derek's father was screaming at the camera crew—pointing in different directions trying to get them to focus on something— anything—else. I could see the veins popping out of his head from my spot in the bleachers. He was red enough to be a sun-spot causing global warming.

I made awkward eye contact with Ellison, who simply shook his head. How did he know I was feeling guilty? Did he know about the bathroom situation after all?

"Yo, Derek isn't going to be cool anymore! Not after that!" "Derek shit his pants again!"

"Just like Becky's house party, man!"

The comments swirled around me. I stared at the brown stained Moby Dick and realized that Thadeous and Aimee were gone. They did do something worse than trading drugs. They rigged the blow up to streak and make it look like Derek shit his pants again.

My mind continued to swirl. How was I going to convince Derek that this wasn't me? I gulped down my thoughts as the gym continued to be in an uproar. There was no settling this disaster quickly. In my mind I kept repeating *save the whales, save the whales, save the whales,* until my heartbeat slowed to normal.

I needed to act now before it was too late. I needed to go to Derek and apologize—not because I was the one who pulled this prank, but because I was genuinely sorry that that just happened to him. No one, including Derek, deserved to be embarrassed like that in front of the entire school. Well, the entire state of Wyoming for that matter.

I peeled away from my spot on the bleachers and went into the hallway. Luckily, it was mostly empty. Everyone was inside the gym roaring with laughter. I made my way down the hallways of Harper towards the parking lot. When I got outside, I could see Derek's father holding Derek by the back of his neck and shoving him into their red pick-up.

Derek wasn't even fighting him. He was going through the motions of being stuffed into the car. His face reminded me of that of his bullying victims—he seriously looked scared in that moment. He looked like the victim. Derek's father successfully stuffed him into the car before I was able to reach them, but not before Derek saw me standing in the middle of the parking lot staring at him.

Great. Now he wasn't going to be able to hear my side of this story. I pulled myself out of the school parking lot faster than a group of baby dinos running from a predator. When I returned to the gym, I was stuck thinking about which noise was worse—the maniacal disorder and laughter that still filled the inside of this stuffy building, or the heavy music that blared from the red car when Derek and his father made their escape.

CON-
CUSSED

The phone begins to ring in Dr. Calian's office, causing me to have to pause my story momentarily. Dr. Calian swivels in his chair away from me and answers the call.

"Harper K-12, Dr. Calian speaking. How may I help you?" There is a long pause as Dr. Calian continues to nod his head. I try to stand slightly, to get a good look at his face. Is he angry? Is he happy? I can't tell. He's doing a good job at making sure I can't see him. "Alright then. I'll see what I can do. Thank you." He hangs up the phone almost dramatically and turns back around to regard me fully. "That was The University of Alabama on the phone. You better continue explaining yourself."

I sigh. Okay. Where was I? And I dive back into the story...

THE DAY AFTER SAVE THE WHALES

The next day I pulled into the parking lot at school and was surprised to see that Allen wasn't waiting at his car for me. That was odd. He's always there, and after the entire fiasco that was "Save the Whales" day, I was hoping that he would be there to provide some moral support.

Where the hell could he be? I was going to scold him for this in Metters' class for sure.

When I got there, he was still missing. The bell rang,

and he was still missing. Metters started his lecture, and he was still missing. Just when I was starting to get concerned about his whereabouts, he and Becky stumbled in freshly blushed and puckered, giggling. I would've said something if Metters didn't step in first.

"Becky Road and Allen, please take your seats to not waste anymore of my time today."

"Awe, how come you still don't say my last name?" Allen whined while sliding into the seat next to me, winking.

"That's enough, Allen. We are starting a new topic today and I hope you all are as excited as I am." Oh, boy. What war was he going to be teaching us about now that I already knew? "You guessed it, The Cold War!" Jesus, that man got way too excited about wars. Maybe he should be a dictator or something. I bet he would be better at that than teaching.

"Psst." My malicious thoughts were interrupted by a rosy-faced Allen. "Do I have the greatest shit to tell you after class." I wanted to slap him hard enough that I didn't have to hear Metters' voice.

"You didn't wait for me in the parking lot today, Al." He blinked twice, as if shaking off an emotional blow.

"I know, I know, but I have a good reason. And I promise you're gonna be excited for me." My childishness taking over, I stopped looking at him to regard Metters at the front of the classroom.

"You didn't wait for me in the parking lot, Allen." I didn't look over at him to see his face.

All I heard was him mumble under his breath—

"Jeeze, why can't you just be happy for me." I wanted to answer him, but I was too focused on the bionic showdown of trees starting outside the window. Those matches were consistent, reliable. Unlike Allen. Except during class that day Little Tree lost. That was the first time Little Tree lost a match.

When the bell rang I rushed out of my seat trying to avoid Allen. I could hear him calling after me but I kept running, and turned the corner right into Derek. He scoffed at me before pushing me away from him. Both his eyes were bruised purple. He was wearing a face of rage, not anger. And I could already tell that he thought yesterday was my fault.

"Gross, Lyle. Don't touch me, I don't want your fat genes on my varsity jacket." Chard laughed while playing with one of the rips in his shirt. He probably didn't have any brain cells left to even back Derek up with a one-liner. "Gotta keep this baby clean so I can sport it at Alabama in the fall." Derek flicked my nose and I slapped his hand. Interesting how he was ignoring the topic altogether— maybe, for once in his life, he was actually embarrassed by something.

"Don't touch me," I said, while taking several steps away from Derek. Allen slid to a halt next to me, followed by Becky.

"Farter's got an attitude today, let's see if he wants a knuckle sandwich?" Derek cocked his fist at my face causing me to flinch and Chard to laugh. A crowd was starting to form around us, as if they actually expected a fight to arise. "Let's go Farter, fucking square up. I still owe you a beating for Becky's party." He pointed a finger to Becky. "That's right, beautiful. It was Farter here that shit all over your bathroom." Ah, there was the blow that I had been waiting for.

"Don't forget you shit yourself yesterday, Derek!" someone in the crowd yelled.

Becky made a disgusted face but didn't say anything. Derek cocked his fist at me again and I slid down into the fetal position to protect myself.

"Don't be a pussy, Farter. Get up!" It seemed like the whole school was watching, and suddenly everything felt slow like a dramatic scene in a movie. I could see Ellison fighting through the crowd to get to the action. Whose side he was on in that moment was a mystery.

Derek grabbed a chunk of my t-shirt and lifted me from the ground. He slammed my entire body into the lockers behind us, causing students to disperse from the area and pull out their phones. Ellison finally got up next to Derek and was trying to pull him from me. Derek shoved him off in one swift motion. "Don't touch me, faggot." Derek looked me in the eyes when he said it, but Ellison shrunk back into the crowd.

Allen was trying to get to me, but Becky was holding him back. Derek finally let go of my shirt and turned to walk away.

"Let this be a warning, Farter. Don't fuck with me again." Derek began to walk away, and the crowd booed. I wanted to keep my mouth shut. I always wanted to keep my mouth shut, but I couldn't.

"I'm not afraid of you, Derek." Derek's body blurred inhumanly as he came running at me. I was vaguely aware of his fist hammered into my face. Once. Twice. Three times. Before I finally lost count. The ringing of my ears could make out the sounds of screaming. I fell to the floor and Allen hovered over me, taking me into his arms. Why was I mad at him again? My brain was feeling a little fuzzy.

The last thing I saw was Dr. Calian pulling Derek away from me and toward his office. Then there was nothing. Just black.

* * *

I woke up in the hospital a couple of hours later. The doctor told me that Karen went to grab a coffee. The doctor also told me that I suffered a minor concussion, but everything was going to be okay. My head was throbbing, and I gulped down enough water to satiate an elephant.

I heard footsteps coming in and was fully expecting Karen to come in and apologize for the awkwardness around the house and shower me with hundreds of mom kisses, but instead it was Ellison who was visiting me. I couldn't hide the shock that was apparent on my face.

"Oh good, you're awake." He pulled up the chair next to my bed and sat down slowly and dignified.

"Were you afraid you would lose your spot at Princeton if you didn't come visit me?"

"You know, Lyle, as much as you might think my whole life is about Princeton, it isn't. I am simply here because I wanted to check on an old friend."

"Old friend, right. Because we aren't friends anymore is that it?" I stared at Ellison through my hazy eyes, drunken by the lack of cohesion in my brain. He let out a sigh.

"Friend, Lyle. You're my friend. That's why I'm here." I started to get up to drink more water, but he stopped me. He poured a new glass and handed it to me instead.

"Is that why you tried to stop Derek?" I was tired of beating around the bush with him. I wanted straight answers.

"Yes, and I was afraid he was going to give you a lot more than a concussion." Ellison paused and nervously wrung out his hands in his lap, a gesture that I had never seen him do, before adding, "I'm sorry I couldn't stop him."

"None of this is your fault, Ellison. I need to learn to stop running my mouth." We laughed.

It hurt my head to laugh. There was one more thing I needed to know before learning to stop running my mouth.

"Why did he say that to you?" Ellison gave me a knowing look. One that said: *Don't ask because then I am going to have to tell you something that I don't want you to know.* But I pushed him anyway. "You know. Why did he call you a f—"

"You don't have to repeat it here." Ellison didn't make direct eye contact with me for what felt like a century. But when he did, I swore there were tears in his eyes. "I'm— I'm gay Lyle, and Derek knows and uses it against me when he wants something." I was floored. Not that Ellison was gay, but that Derek would stoop so low.

"How come you never told me?"

"I'm black and gay in this small ass town. It would be all everyone would talk about. I didn't even tell Derek. He found out because he read my journal." I rubbed my eyes a couple of times hoping it would provide some sort of clarity. I must have been taking too long because Ellison was getting nervous. "Lyle?" Right, now is the time to say something consoling.

"I get it now, you stopped hanging out with me because you had a crush on me!" The air was tense, and I expected to get punched in the face for the second time today, but Ellison laughed.

He laughed so hard that he started crying. He was wiping the tears from the corners of his eyes with a nearby tissue.

"Leave it to you to make a joke at a time like this, Lyle. You ain't even my type."

Then I was laughing. I laughed and laughed until I forgot about the pain in my head. I let myself settle down for a minute.

"But seriously, Ellison. I don't care who you like. The only thing that bothers me is the fact that Derek is an asshole." Ellison gave a different look this time. One that said: *Thank you.*

We talked for a little while longer before Karen came and kicked him out. She didn't apologize for the awkwardness around the house, but she did shower me with hundreds of kisses.

BATTER
(KAREN) UP

I spent the rest of the week lying in bed staring at my ceiling. I had become so familiar with each bump, scratch, and dent in my walls that I could create a new mapping of the stars. My own mini constellations. It was the highest I could see after all, and as far as I was concerned it was as good as the night sky.

Karen would come to visit me every now and then. She would bring me food, but I couldn't keep most of it down. Eventually, around Friday afternoon, my head finally stopped throbbing, and I was feeling much less concussed than when Derek decided to pummel my face over some shit (literally). I knew shit hit the fan that night, but I hadn't realized just how badly things were going to become. All over a bowl of chili and a high school prank. Damn.

The thing that bothered me the most was the fact that I haven't heard from Allen since that day at school. He hadn't texted me, called, or even attempted to visit (Karen wasn't letting anyone in because I needed "rest" and to "think about what I had done"). I wanted to blame Allen not visiting on Becky, but it "takes two to bake a pie" or whatever people say, so that meant Allen was just as guilty. Or maybe I was just as guilty? I hadn't tried to call him either.

I picked up my phone and shot him a quick text...

> Hey, Al. Finally feeling
> better Prob be back to
> school Monday. Meet you in
> the parking lot?

I saw the ... of him beginning to text back for a couple of minutes, but then they disappeared. I redirected my anger towards iPhones for allowing people to see when others change their minds about wanting to text you back. Allen better have the best excuse for ignoring me. Especially when I needed him.

By the time Karen got home, I had migrated downstairs and was sitting on the couch. The doctor at the hospital told me I shouldn't be staring at screens because it would be bad for the recovery of my brain, but I figured since I was feeling better it wouldn't hurt. Plus, *Jurassic World* was on. I wasn't a huge fan of the newer movies. It was never about them being bad, more about me being a pretentious movie-goer who was stuck with his vintage attitude, but as long as dinosaurs were involved, I was at peace with it.

Karen was holding take out bags, and suddenly I felt hungry. Like I was starving myself for an entire week. Well, I guess it was because I was starving myself for an entire week. Not on purpose though. Karen didn't say anything. She just went to the kitchen and grabbed some bowls, plates, and forks. I reluctantly followed her and sat down at the table.

After talking there with Dr. Calian and failing to convince Karen to let us borrow the car to drive to Yellowstone, the table felt more like the scene of a historic battleground than a place where we were supposed to sit down and enjoy dinner. But then again, this table always felt distant without Larry sitting at it. My mind was beginning to travel to a dark place—

What if this table really was a battlefield? What if, after all the lessons I have learned on WWII, it was coming to life right in front of my eyes? The tablecloth battered against the hardwood like the ships in the seas of D-Day. I would be exiting the boat soon to storm the beaches, and if I wasn't careful I would die there. Karen didn't look the type to pull the trigger, but in times of war you had to do what you could to survive.

Karen's voice pulled me back to reality.

"Lyle." I looked up to her with a dumpling half hanging out of my mouth.

"Karen." I wanted to talk to her like I always did. I wanted some aspect of my life, my body, to feel normal. She huffed before answering.

"Mom—How are you feeling?" She sighed after asking me, almost saying: *I do care how you are feeling, but I am tired of your shit.*

"Much better. I think I am going to go back to school on Monday. And I am definitely going to see Dr. Calian tomorrow. He sent me an email saying he had good news for me." Another sigh.

"You were on your computer even though the doctor told you to stay away from screens?" Her tone of voice hadn't sounded mad anymore. Instead it held a hint of defeat. Almost like her vocal cords were struggling to put together anything remotely close to emotion.

"I got the email to my phone. I was honestly hoping that I would hear from Allen, but I didn't." Karen was pushing around her Chinese food on her plate. I realized that she hadn't even touched her food.

"Two strikes, Lyle."

I stared at her confused. "What?"

"Two strikes. That's how many you have right now. One being you throwing a temper tantrum like a child instead of acting like an eighteen-year-old young man. Two being you egging on a fellow student so much so that they felt the need to shut your mouth." She paused as if to gather her thoughts before continuing. I could tell by the look on her face that she was perfectly calculating each word she said in her mind before allowing the utterances to reach her lips. "I have been so patient with you. Understanding and patient. But—I'm at my limit. One more strike Lyle, and well—you don't want to even begin to fathom what will happen then."

Karen rose from the table and began to leave. She turned around to add: "Also, Lyle. You need to stop relying on Allen for everything. That boy isn't going to be here to pick you up every time you fall. It seems to me like Allen is starting to grow up. Maybe you should take some advice from him." With that she left to go upstairs.

I sat alone at the kitchen table. How did she know anything about Allen? And when did she start considering our relationship to be the equivalent to a game of baseball? I could only sit there and imagine what thoughts were going through her head. I was having trouble even sifting through my own.

The one thing I was sure of: *I was still on the offensive.* I had two strikes and God knows how many balls. But I could still make this right. I could still hit it out of the park.

* * *

Karen had already left the next morning when I got up. She left a note saying:

Girl's day—be back later.

I wasn't sure what a girl's day was, but I had thoughts like manicures and blow outs and suddenly I found myself picking my nails. She left her car for me to go see Dr. Calian.

Normally hesitant, I flew outside to the car and recklessly drove over to the school. Dr. Calian had good news for me. And I needed to know. If any velociraptors were crossing the street today, I would've mowed them down.

When I got into Dr. Calian's office he wasn't there, and I allowed my over-boisterous attitude to get the best of me and I snooped through his office. That was the first time that I had looked through your things. I was about to give up having only found a mummified candy under his desk when I noticed something more interesting lying on top of a handful of sprawled out papers. Rather, two interesting things.

1. A sticky note with the phone number to the University of Alabama and two words—*lost scholarship*. And—

2. Chard's file.

Both were tantalizing. The first note can only mean one thing—Derek must have lost his scholarship to play football because he assaulted me on school grounds. Pfft—and Karen thinks that was my fault. I felt utterly satisfied at the world. Karma really did bite his ass. Or, at the very least, Karma was beginning to straighten some things out.

The second, Chard's file, was much more secretive. I opened it and found something that I wasn't expecting.

Chard's grades were actually amazing. A's in every subject except math, which, let's face it, everyone hates math so that was understandable. But he still held a solid B+ in math. His date of birth was 1999 making him nineteen. That meant he was indeed supposed to graduate a year before us. But if his grades were so good, then why was he still there? Why was he sticking around in Wyoming?

Just as I was about to get the answers I deliciously desired, I heard the turning of a door handle. I snapped back into my body and jumped into the seat set out for me to avoid suspicion. The last thing I needed was to get caught snooping. For all I knew, something as little as that could be enough to earn my third strike from Karen.

Dr. Calian looked crisp as usual. He was smiling a huge smile and was holding an even bigger envelope.

"Good morning, Lyle." He handed the envelope to me. It was from The University of Wyoming and it had my name on it. "I called the school and asked for this personally. I know that I am usually not supposed to interfere with students' college letters, but I made a special exception for you, so you could receive it as soon as possible. Go on. Open it."

The thick envelope began to sweat in my palms. I peeled back the flap and watched the glue peel from each side cobwebbing in the middle. It opened much like the letter that Larry left me. But since I was no longer allowed to think about that, I buried it deep into my mind and focused on my new task. The envelope's contents were unfamiliar, but positive. I was accepted. And into their honors program. I looked up to Dr. Calian to make sure this wasn't another one of my visions.

"Maybe you should go home and tell your mom, but first how are you feeling?" How was I feeling? Derek lost his scholarship. Chard was smart despite faking. Allen was probably getting laid, and I got into college. I was stunned into silence. Stunned into a new feeling—wonderment. My silence seemed to alarm Dr. Calian—in a good way.

"Go home, Lyle. We will talk more next weekend." Dr. Calian was barely able to finish his sentence before I ran out of his office. I drove home even more erratically than I drove to school. They should take my license away, truly.

Karen still wasn't home, so I decided to reward myself with the diner downtown. I even texted Ellison to meet me there so I could tell him the news. I wasn't sure which news I was going to tell him first because there was too much juicy shit to go over.

When I pulled into the diner, I went right inside to meet Ellison. He wasn't there yet. I was waiting by the hostess stand and letting my eyes wander from the Key Lime Pie to the Boston Crème Pie to Karen and Uncle Danny to the croissants. Wait. I had to slow my mind to register what I was witnessing.

Karen wasn't having a girl's day. She was there, at the diner, with Uncle Danny. But why?

There were only so many secrets that my mind could handle for one day. I ran out of the diner and right into Ellison. I grabbed onto his arm and pulled him behind me.

"Can't explain right now, come with me." Ellison was stunned as I dragged him over to Karen's car. Ellison hopped into the passenger seat as I darted inside.

"Jesus, Lyle! Would you slow down? You are just

coming off of a concussion and you need to take it easy!" Ellison was able to remain the voice of reason even during the most chaotic of times. "I thought you wanted to get food?"

"I changed my mind. Let's just grab some snacks at my house." I turned the car on and began to drive away.

"Lyle! Wait! My car's here!" I forgot that Ellison drove to meet me here. My brain was too frazzled to make educated decisions.

"Right! I'll take you back later to get it." I took off wildly in the car for the third time today. My mind was stuffed full like a turkey on Thanksgiving. There was no more room left to process information.

Max capacity. Error. Error.

I pulled into my driveway to see that Allen and Becky were waiting outside of my house. Overload. Abort mission.

I jumped out of the car and stomped over to Allen. Part of me wanted to hit him. Part of me wanted to jump into his arms like an eager lover. I settled for somewhere in the middle.

"Allen," I said platonically.

"Jesus Christ, Lyle! Where have you been? Actually— no, don't answer that, there's no time. You two need to come with us!" My brain had finally turned into sludge, and I couldn't form words or adequate thoughts anymore.

"You all need to calm down," the Voice of Reason said. "Now, why do we need to come with you?"

"Long story short, Becky and I were in the old arcade in town and we found it," Loud Boy answered.

"You found what exactly?" inquired the Voice of Reason.

"The clue, duh!" Sassy girl spoke finally.

"The clue?" Mush Brain said and thought in third-person. "Seriously, Lyle? Becky and I found the second clue to your letter!"

CRETACEOUS FOREST TRIED
Ṭ̱₀ RIP OFF JURASSIC PARK

I gathered together my thoughts enough to register what Allen had just said to me. The second clue—something that I had abandoned all hope of finding, and something that I was forbidden to pursue by both Karen and Dr. Calian—was nipping at my ankles. Begging to be solved once again. The mush that was once my brain solidified back into a fully formed thinking machine. I was ready to do cartwheels and handstands across my lawn. That day had been equally amazing as it was bizarre. Finally, the party I was throwing inside my skull was broken by the Voice of Reason, well—Ellison.

"How are you sure that you found the second clue?" Always accurate and always quizzical, Ellison left Allen speechless. The hope I felt was starting to disappear.

"Look." Becky's unexpected voice answered my thoughts. "You wanted me to trust you in the beginning, and I will admit that I was a little apprehensive, but I can promise you all that this is legit. Allen and I were in the arcade making—making plans to study when we ran into each other at the arcade. And well, the rest you are just going to have to see for yourselves!" Becky huffed and turned away in embarrassment. If she thought that Ellison and I didn't know about her and Allen, she was sillier than I thought. But that didn't stop me from wanting to antagonize the situation.

"What were you and Allen doing together in the arcade in the first place, hm?" Ellison snickered beside me which caused us both to have to stifle our laughter.

"Damnit, Lyle, that's not what's important right now!" Allen yelled loud enough to startle us back into proper behavior. "Are you coming with us or not?" I'd made up my mind before Allen even had to ask that question.

"Of course. Show us the way!" The car ride over to the arcade was easily one of the most awkward things I had ever experienced. More awkward than getting a boner in class. The silence was silent enough that my own thoughts echoed through the vehicle. Allen was whipped more than cream into keeping his relationship with Becky a secret. He couldn't even tell his best buddy.

Why was she so adamant about keeping it a secret anyway? I mean, Allen is easy on the eyes, so what gives? I guessed that Becky has her secrets too, just like Chard and Karen.

Everyone in town was smaller than a grain of sand, and they were much more interesting than I ever thought they were.

We pulled into the arcade parking lot just in time. I was about to throw myself out the car door just to escape the awkwardness, but when we pulled up everything dissipated into excitement. We all unbuckled our seatbelts and headed inside. Ellison and I didn't know where we were going, so we had to follow the leader. We weaved around Asteroids, made a left by Pac Man, a right by Donkey Kong, and finally pulled up in front of a game that I don't remember becoming mainstream.

The sides of the large console were covered in all different types of dinosaurs. They ranged from a

Stegosaurus, to a Triceratops, to a Velociraptor, and finally a T-Rex. The game was called Cretaceous Forest—which I am assuming is supposed to be a rip off of *Jurassic Park*. I was starting to get suspicious that Allen was simply making connections to the letter because he saw dinosaurs out of the corner of his eye while he was playing tonsil hockey with Becky.

"Hey, Lyle? Remember when we did all that research in the library?" Ellison questioned as I took a few more steps towards the game to look at its terribly pixelated graphics. "How the Tyrannosaurus Rex actually lived during the Cretaceous period, not the Jurassic?" Ellison was onto something. Hollywood let the mainstream public believe that the Jurassic Period was the home of the T-Rex, but Larry would've known the truth.

"That's not all Lyle, look!" The screen flashed from some small eating dinosaurs to a gold coin. The screen flashed over and over again—GO FOR GOLD.

It took me a moment to catch my breath. It was real. It was really happening. It wasn't velociraptors crossing the street in my mind. It was something I could reach out and grab. Something that Larry left behind for me to find.

"Well, what's the clue?" Ellison asked.

"We got so excited when we saw it we rushed right over to get you guys." I wasn't sure what was more surprising—actually finding the clue, or that fact that Becky was actually excited about something that involved the project.

"What do we do now, Lyle?" All three of them looked at me for the answer, and to me it was simple.

"We play." We each took turns playing the game, which in spite of its terrible graphics, was actually really difficult. The game's premise was that a person (the player) was in an airplane when it crashed into a forest that somehow (not explained in the game which was a major plot hole in my opinion) was filled with dinosaurs. One rascal of a dinosaur stole a gold coin from the player (which means a lot to him because it was given to him by his deceased father—so I could relate). The objective of the game was to get the coin back. Oh, and survive of course.

The game was difficult, though. The controls weren't straight forward, and the terrain was hard to maneuver. We spent most of the twenty dollars we had between us getting eaten or falling off of cliffs. And the dinos were ruthless in that game—as they should be.

The T-Rex didn't show up until the final level of the game and he easily killed us eight times. We only had one quarter left and it was Becky's turn. Great. The whole rest of the journey lay on the shoulders of someone who had JUST decided they found the project interesting. I almost wanted to propose someone else do it, but Becky had a determined look in her eyes, and I just had to trust her.

The game started as always. Once the backstory finished Becky dove right in killing all the dinos in her path. She was ruthless. We all looked at her in awe. Especially Allen. He looked like a proud boyfriend, except he wasn't. Becky was too good at this game for it to be the first time she was playing it. That, or she was a secret videogame fiend and just hid it well. I always knew she was a nerd anyway.

She got to the final stage and used all the ammo she had left on the T-Rex. All three of us were screaming behind her, chanting her name, and grabbing onto her shoulders. She didn't let our antics distract her though.

She was on a mission. Even the arcade worker stalked out to watch her annihilate the T-Rex and claim what was rightfully hers—gold.

The character in the game walked up and shot the rascal dinosaur from the beginning. The character snatched up the gold coin before thrusting it into the air in sheer victory. A war cry was heard over the game as the screen faded to black. We all stared, waiting for the second clue to reveal itself, but the screen went back to start demanding another quarter to be played again. I could feel all of our hearts sink into the floor. Time seemed to stop in that moment of sheer disappointment. This wasn't the second clue after all—just a coincidence.

I was ready to sulk home when Becky flew around and stormed up to the arcade worker.

"What the hell, man! Where's our prize? We just played this damn game for two hours for what? A half-assed orgasm-like scream? No way! Where's the second clue, buster?" The arcade worker was easily a grandfather. His one ear sported a hearing aid, and what was left of his thinning hair was white. I almost felt bad that Becky was screaming at him, but all he did was smile.

"You four are the first kids to ever beat that game." He even sounded sweet. He also sounded like he was about to reminisce about how kids used to play arcade games all the time, but then cellphones came out and corrupted everyone—and I wanted to avoid that trip down memory lane.

"Do we get anything for winning? A free soda maybe?" I wanted to keep the bargain low without pressing our luck. I wanted the second clue just as badly as everyone else here. Becky's style, however, was much more forceful.

"No! We want the clue!" The old arcade worker sauntered off without another word.

Probably because he didn't want to be screamed at by a bunch of bratty kids anymore. It took everything in my being not to rip Becky's face off right then and there. Just when I thought about simply pulling her hair instead, the old arcade worker opened up a closed door and motioned for us to follow him. We all looked at each other and shrugged. We had nothing else to lose at that point.

The room that the arcade worker took us into looked like an office, except it also looked like my bedroom—like a bomb went off and it hadn't been cleaned for eighteen years. The old arcade worker was opening and closing a bunch of cabinets mumbling to himself.

"Now, I am sure it is back in here somewhere." He opened a jar and threw some cookies out of it which hit the wall with unimaginable force. Becky was stomping her foot next to me, growing impatient.

"Hey," Allen whispered, "give the guy a chance." Becky squeezed Allen's hand.

"I know, this is just, ugh!" Becky suppressed her urge to throw a full-on bitch fit in the small office.

"Here it is!" We all turned to look at the old arcade worker with huge eyes. "No—no, that's my medical statement from last month. I really need to get new glasses."

"Uh, sir? Is there anything we can do to help?" I tried to hide the fact that I was just as impatient as Becky in that moment.

"A very nice young man gave it to me. I just have to remember where I put it. Gold, gold, I'm looking for something gold." A nice young man? He must be talking about Larry! The arcade worker opened up what felt like the last drawer in the room and pulled out an envelope. "Ah, yes! Here it is. You know, you kind of look like him, much thinner though," he said while he handed the letter over to me. "I have been waiting quite some time to give out this letter, that is why I misplaced it. He did say there would only be one." The *he* that the old arcade worker must be talking about is Larry. Larry must have set up an agreement with the arcade before he died. This was so much more involved than I imagined.

We all thanked him, even Becky, before returning to Allen's car to open the clue. All it said was—

L,

Great Job! You're almost there! Here
is the second clue—
Frogs sing at night
Dinosaurs roam by
day.

That clue was more straightforward. I knew what it was right away. I knew I wasn't supposed to keep hunting for that skeleton. I knew I should go home and accept my acceptance to The University of Wyoming, become a writer, write amazing novels filled with all the things that take up my imagination, and hell—even win prizes. I knew that is what I should do. But it wasn't what I wanted. Allen, Ellison, and Becky stared flabbergasted at the note.

"I know what it means," I told them, making up my mind about my future and the consequences that might come with it. "And I can take you there right now."

BONES ARE BONES TILL
THEY SING LIKE FOSSILS

Allen let me drive his car to the next spot. That was honestly a bad decision on his part, but I wasn't complaining. And it was getting dark out. We needed to find the next clue before the sun went down and preferably before Karen got home from her secret rendez-vous with Uncle Danny. I was too much in the zone during the drive to see anything but the road that led us to our next destination.

I drove the four of us over to the old stream I visited when I was coincidentally avoiding Uncle Danny. Uncle Danny would come here with us sometimes to go fishing. I guess nothing in life really is a coincidence then.

When we pulled up to the old stream, I started to think about one time that I came here with Larry and Uncle Danny...

I was playing with the weeds near the old hollowed out tree when I heard a frog croaking. It was loud, but muffled, like it was hiding inside of something. I followed the noise closer to the tree. Inside the tree was a frog all by itself croaking. The frog looked sad and lonely.

I climbed inside the tree and picked up the frog and sat it inside my lap. I sat there stroking his back with two fingers. It cooed underneath my middle and index. It wasn't alone anymore. Maybe I was humming, maybe I wasn't. I don't remember. I heard Larry and Uncle Danny screaming for me, but I stayed with the frog.

It took me a moment to realize that while I was remembering my past I was actually moving on autopilot in real time. I put Allen's car into park and began walking over to the hollowed out tree. Allen, Becky, and Ellison were all following behind me. The tree was too big for me to squeeze into now, but I was small enough to reach my arm in and feel around.

I mostly felt sap, leaves, and probably bugs, but I told myself they were acorns to avoid panicking.

When Larry and Uncle Danny found me inside the tree stump, they pulled me out aggressively causing me to hit my head. I started crying right away—not because my head hurt, but because I was upset that they were taking me away from my new friend. I told Larry I didn't want to leave my frog because it wouldn't have anyone to hum to it. Larry responded—

"Even when this frog is lonely, it will always be able to sing to itself, Lyle. Just remember— dinosaurs used to roam here, and their bones sing sometimes too."

My fingers came into contact with something plastic and I yanked. I pulled out an old- yellowed Ziploc bag that had a note inside with the letter L.

I used to believe that dinosaur bones really could sing you to sleep, but then I realized that it was just something that Larry told me so I would leave the frog. That frog was probably long dead by now—maybe even a fossil itself. I wasn't sure anymore if dinosaur bones, or frog bones for that matter, could sing, but they could help you remember things that you had forgotten.

As my mind was full of the past a single voice shattered my memories and pulled me back into the present.

"Is that it, Lyle?" Allen asked. Three sets of eyes

lingered on me as I smiled a toothy T-Rex grin.

"You bet it is!" I said while carefully taking the letter out of its protective yet temporary tomb. The letter read:

L,

S.S. knew the devil didn't fall here, but he was wrong about the life that could be found—This is the last clue. Seek answers and the skeleton is yours.

I read the letter a couple of times out loud to everyone, but each time the letter got more confusing. Who was S.S.? What kind of life did he or she think could be found here and why were they wrong?

Too many questions piled into my single brain. So much so that my mind could only fathom them into a messy-brain list:

1. Did Derek really lose his scholarship?
2. What's up with Chard?
3. Will Becky ever let Allen in?
4. Why is Karen sneaking around with Uncle Danny?
5. What the actual fuck does this last clue mean?

Just as I was about to rip the paper in half and give up on all of Wyoming, Allen peeled the letter from me wearing a shit-eating grin.

"I can't believe it," he said, "You don't know what this last clue means, do you?" I wanted to slap him for being cocky. For a moment, the hollowed out tree began to turn bionic behind Allen. Ready and willing to throw hands—or tree limbs.

"No, why don't you enlighten us, Allen?" Ellison stopped the hollowed out tree from carrying out a full-on assault on Allen.

"Well," he began, "thinking in terms of what we already know about this adventure— *Jurassic Park* is a main component, being it's about dinosaurs and all and that's where the first clue was found. Anyway—*Jurassic Park* was produced by Steven Spielberg—or S.S. Another HUGELY famous film by him, which honestly you guys, how you don't know this considering we are all nerds here is beyond me, but anyway—is *Close Encounters of the Third Kind*!"

"What does that have to do with dinosaurs—it's about aliens isn't it? And don't put me in your nerd boat, Allen," Becky interrupted.

"First of all, considering you know what a Scify movie is about proves you are indeed a nerd, my dear Becky. Second of all, aren't aliens 'the kind of life' that could have lived there just like the letter says?" Allen rebutted.

"So what's the clue then?" Ellison asked as Becky crossed her arms and pouted over being proven to be a nerd.

"Devils Tower plays a huge role in the film. Hello, you guys! Devils Tower is in Wyoming."

About an hour northeast from here. My parents took me there when I was a kid. Everything makes sense. That's where the dinosaur is, Lyle!" Everything Allen was saying was plausible. Larry loved everything by Steven Spielberg. He could've easily made the connection between the two films.

"Okay, but let's watch that movie next weekend just to be sure," I added. The sun was finally almost down, and I needed to get home before Karen. "Let's talk more about this in the car."

We all started walking back, but Ellison tapped on my shoulder which caused me to jump a little.

"What was Allen talking about, you finding the letter inside *Jurassic Park*? And if the clue really is Devils Tower then we should've done my idea from the beginning!" Shit. Ellison continued to stare at me while I was having a mental breakdown. I had completely forgotten for a moment that Ellison and Becky were still in the dark about how I came about the letter in the first place. Ellison had been so nice since the beginning, and Becky fought it, so if I were to tell them now that Larry was involved, they might pull out. Or worse. Maybe they would tell Karen. And then Karen would start asking a bunch of questions that I wouldn't be able to answer. I could feel it being strike three already.

Ellison continued to stare at me as I found out the right way to lie to him about this.

"I don't know," I said, "I think that Allen got a little excited in his explanation there." Ellison shook his head. He wasn't buying it.

"Lyle, you know you can tell me right?" Could I? I mean, he did know Larry when he was alive, but could I really admit everything to him? Could I say: *Hell yeah man, I found this dusty letter and map with my late father's things and just assumed that it was legit?* He wouldn't believe me. There was no way.

"I know. But seriously, I have no idea what Allen was talking about." I knew that wasn't going to be enough to convince Mr. Princeton. But he didn't push me further. At one point or another I was going to have to admit to

Ellison and Becky the truth.

Or maybe not. Maybe when we found the skeleton everything would be forgotten. All the second guessing and Karen denying us. Hell, Karen would probably be kissing my feet then, and all of us would be rich. I could see the headlines: LOCAL TEENS UNEARTH CRETACEOUS BEAST. Yes. Yes. Everything was going to work out perfectly. All we had to do now was watch the Alien movie to get a sense of what Devils Tower was like.

The car ride back to my house was mostly silent. I for one was exhausted, and I was sure that everyone else was as well. When we pulled into my driveway, Ellison and I were getting out of Allen's car when Becky spoke up.

"You guys can come over to my house next Friday to watch that movie. I think my parents own it." Becky was twirling her hair awkwardly. "But only if you bring snacks." I couldn't believe that Becky Road was actually personally inviting our goon squad to her house to watch a science fiction classic. What was happening to this little town?

"Cool, when should we come over?" Allen was quick to accept her invitation. Probably because this could be one step closer to her actually letting him into her life. I couldn't help but feel like a proud father in that moment. My baby was growing up.

"Come at seven, but with snacks guys, I'm serious." With that Allen retook his position in the driver's seat and they left. I hopped into Karen's car to drive Ellison back to the diner where his car was waiting for him.

Lucky for me, Ellison didn't pry me with questions like earlier. The good thing about Ellison being uber smart was that he knew when other people weren't going to cooperate with him. The bad thing about Ellison being uber smart was that he knew that I was lying to him. And no matter how silent he was, one day he was going to break that.

I left Ellison just as the sun was about to sleep for the night. I knew that Karen was going to be home, so I had to come up with some excuse as to why I wasn't there. When I got home, Karen was sitting at the kitchen table waiting for me. Damn.

She had made what looked like meatloaf and mashed potatoes, which was funny because I knew that she had eaten with Uncle Danny. She was really trying hard to cover for herself. But I was going to play coy. If I was keeping secrets from Karen it seemed only fair for her to be keeping secrets from me.

"Karen," I said, "How was your girl's day?"

"Lovely. I got a manicure. Do you wanna see?" Lie. But I fed into it.

"Of course." I leaned forward to see that she did indeed get her nails done. They were slathered and glossed in an ugly puke green color, but I didn't have the heart to tell her that.

"Looks good," I lied.

"Where were you all day?" Showtime. Time to put all the drama classes I never took to use. "Well I went to see Dr. Calian today who gave me my acceptance letter to The University of

Wyoming." I paused to see if she was going to do some mom thing like cry, but she didn't, so I decided to continue. I knew this was a test that I was going to pass. "Then after that I wanted to celebrate with my friends, so I called up Allen, Ellison, and Becky and we went and hung out at the arcade for the rest of the day." Okay, most of that story was the truth. But Karen still had a look in her eye suggesting that she was trying to poke holes in my story.

"You really are getting along with them well, huh?" I was surprised that Karen was talking about my friends rather than me getting into college. She was being weird.

"Yeah, Karen. I am as surprised as you are." I forced a laugh that felt fake the moment it left my mouth. The fact that I needed to pretend with my own mother bothered me. I wanted to be able to have a relationship with her— one where I could tell her anything. But ever since Larry died, neither of us had been willing to be open about our feelings. We both built a wall around ourselves, and sometimes I was sure that Karen's wall was much higher than my own.

"That's good. And I'm glad you got into UW. Do you think you'll go?" I stared, determined, back at her. I had done everything she asked of me. Why wasn't she more excited? What more could she possibly want? How would I ever be able to prove to her that I was worthy when she wasn't even giving me a fair chance at bat?

"Well, I got a full ride, so maybe." She smiled. Finally.

"Want some meatloaf?" After everything that my brain had to process today the last thing I thought about then was food.

"No thank you. I am actually pretty tired, so I'm gonna head to bed. Night night, Karen." Another lie. I wasn't tired at all, but it took my body longer than usual to get up the stairs. It was like my brain forgot how to use my legs. When I finally got there, I settled in front of my mirror to take in my dashing looks. My black hair was a shaggy mess as usual, but my eye bags were large enough to pass as designer. I looked exhausted, but I didn't feel it. No. I felt something that I hadn't felt in a long time. Hope.

ALIENS ARE
COOL, TOO

The next week went by in a hazy blur that consisted of me mildly stalking Chard and avoiding Derek although he was still suspended for beating me up. I guess old habits did indeed die hard like the old folks say.

Chard's life was exceptionally boring, though, especially without Derek around. I always knew that Derek was the chief antagonizer in our small school, but I hadn't realized that his absence would bring such peace to the hallways. Not a single freshman was struggling to get their locker unglued and no one was walking around prying an unnatural wedgie out from between their cheeks. I wondered why it took the school so long to step up and suspend him. I guessed they assumed no harm no foul, but when someone ended up in the hospital they had to take some sort of precaution.

Classes were as boring as usual. Mr. Metters was still on his Cold War fix, which was fitting considering it felt like it hadn't stopped snowing here in weeks. That's a normal mid- March for here though. Cold, bitter, and lonely. Exceptionally lonely. Allen was still in his love- sick craze of sneaking away with Becky, so I had no one to hang out with after school besides Ellison, but I was still avoiding him because he knew my secret about Larry.

All in all, when Friday finally rolled around, I was getting sick of watching the fighter jets freeze in mid-air outside the classroom windows, and I was actually ready to get together with my friends to watch the movie. I wasn't sure what to expect, or if I was going to actually get any answers from it, but it was the best lead we had, and I wasn't about to walk away from that.

On the way home from school I stopped at The Market to pick up some snacks. Becky was very firm about us bringing something, and she was being nice enough to let us use her home for our viewing party. Although Allen and I had watched *Jurassic Park* a couple of weeks ago, I was still a little rusty on what kind of snacks were appropriate for a viewing party.

Whenever it was me, Larry, and Allen, we would always have a full pizza, but that wasn't a snack so much as it was a meal, so I was going to have to skip out on that. Becky and Ellison didn't strike me as the type who would like to slurp on some Mountain Dews and munch on Doritos, so I was officially at a loss. Gluten free snacks were lame. And anything with the word wheat in it gave me the heeby-geebies, so that was a no go.

Pacing back and forth in The Market felt like a bad look for me, so I folded and stuck to what I knew best. Mountain Dew and Doritos it was. Becky did say to bring snacks; she didn't mention that she was on a health kick or anything which made me feel less guilty.

When I got home, Karen wasn't there. She was either at work still or having another secret tryst with Uncle Danny. Either way, it meant she wasn't there to judge my every movement and give me a strike three for accidentally leaving the toilet seat up or something stupid. I sat around until 7 rolled up and Allen pulled into my driveway. He leaned on his horn obnoxiously to let me know he was here. I pulled on my Chucks and met him outside.

It didn't take long for me to realize that he looked different. Aside from his hair being groomed immensely, he had ditched his glasses for what I could only assume were contacts.

"Al, you look handsome as hell. Did you get all dressed up just for me?" I couldn't help teasing him as I slid into the passenger seat.

"Oh, Lyle. You know I could only pull myself together this much for you." He paused to give me a dopey grin. "But seriously, do I look weird without my glasses or do I look like a stud?" He wiggled his eyebrows which caused me to laugh. Not because it was funny, but because he was a train wreck.

"I already told you you look handsome, you weirdo." Allen backed out of my driveway to drive the three blocks to Becky's house. Ideally, we could've walked like I did the last time, but one it was too cold outside, and my boogers would freeze, and two it brought back bad memories of me having to escape Becky's party. "But seriously, Al. Do you think that trading in your glasses is going to make Becky budge on the relationship front?"

"Look." I must've struck a chord because Allen's voice turned serious when he answered me. "I know you are just trying to look out for me, but I got this okay?" I wanted to believe him with all of my heart, but there was something still holding me back. Some primal urge to protect my best friend at all costs.

"I know, I was just concerned because you haven't been around much lately," I said honestly. "I've been around," Allen answered without taking his eyes off the road.

"Well, I mean, you haven't been around to hang out with me I meant." I didn't want to sound possessive, but I knew I came off that way.

"If I am being honest, Lyle, it's because I am having trouble balancing my time. I've never been in this situation before, but I promise I'm not ignoring you on purpose. I am just getting used to this new relationship." Allen called it a relationship, but I was still unsure that Becky was calling it the same thing, and that bothered me. I suppressed my urge to say anything else just in time for us to make it to Becky's.

Ellison was already there, so we grabbed our snacks and headed in. Allen didn't ring the doorbell, which made me think that he had been here on multiple occasions. Maybe he did have this. Something that Karen said was starting to boil up in my memory. Something along the lines of Allen growing up and becoming mature while I wasn't. Maybe Karen was right. But being mature was for weenies anyway.

We found Ellison and Becky in the kitchen idly chatting over some chips. Becky was sipping on a drink when we walked in and she almost choked. She was looking right at Allen. Damn. He was right. The contacts were a hit. Becky looked beautiful in that moment. Like she had finally seen something more interesting than jewelry walk through her front door.

"Y-you guys better have brought snacks!" she stammered. I had never seen Becky lose a step in her life. All over a guy. All over Allen at that. It was truly a wonderful sight.

"We brought Mountain Dew and Doritos, hope that's

okay," Allen said while sauntering over to the table to place everything down.

"That's perfect. Actually, don't put those there. We can bring them right into the basement." Becky scampered off towards the door to the basement and we followed. I winked at Ellison who was laughing into the collar of his shirt. I already knew that night was going to be interesting, but I hadn't realized the entertainment was going to be coming from somewhere other than the movie.

Being in Becky's basement was strange. I was used to my old black leather porn couch and big backed TV, but Becky's basement was something else. It was almost a small theater. There were exactly four seats, ones that reclined when you pushed a button on the side. The arms in between the seats even lifted up, so you could steal some snuggle time if you chose too. And the TV was huge. Well over sixty-four inches huge. I couldn't help but feel a little jealous. And it smelt like lavender; the perfect touch.

"The movie is already in the DVD player. I forgot something upstairs. You guys can start it without me. I'll be right back." Becky started to turn to go back upstairs before adding, "Allen, actually can you help me a minute?"

Allen didn't hesitate to get up and practically ran after Becky. They slid up the stairs like two slippery otters who were dancing in the water together. Perfectly in love, perfectly open about it.

"Why do you think they keep their relationship a secret?" The words spilled out of my mouth before I even had the chance to realize what I was saying. Ellison looked at me with a stern face. One similar to a face that Karen would give me for asking a stupid question.

"You're talking to someone who hides their sexuality.

We all have our reasons, Lyle."

Ellison's response stung and I openly flinched at his words. It was almost like taking an emotional bullet. He wasn't just talking about the fact that he was gay and hiding it. He was still holding the fact over my head that I wasn't telling him the truth about our project. His stern eyes turned tender. "I'm sorry, Lyle. That was out of place. I think I meant that they will come around. I mean they are pretty open just around us."

I was still shaking off the awkwardness from Ellison's original reply. But I was regaining the playfulness I felt when I was teasing Allen in the car.

"I bet Becky didn't even leave anything upstairs, she just wanted to dig her dirty claws through Allen's freshly combed locks." Ellison laughed at my inquiry.

"You're probably right. We should give them some time."

"Hell nah, this might be the ONLY chance in my life that I get to cockblock him. I'm taking it." I started up the stairs and instead of protesting, Ellison followed. We made our way into the kitchen to see Becky hoisted up on the table with her legs wrapped around Allen's waist. They were so busy attacking each other's faces that they didn't even realize we had come upstairs.

That moment was almost too great for words. I didn't think Allen had it in him. Gawking started to feel awkward so I decided it was time to make it more awkward.

"Hey!" My voice caused a rift between the two, and they jumped apart from one another. Their faces were redder than what you would receive from a harsh wind. "Your booty is crushing my Doritos." I pointed at the table. Well, we really did forget something, but that didn't stop that moment from being too good. Instead of being the gushy mess she was when Allen first walked into her house, Becky started laughing uncontrollably.

It was infectious because we all started laughing too. It was an uncontained laughter that filled Becky's kitchen. My stomach actually started to hurt. For a moment I started to think that was what it felt like to have real friends. I was feeling sentimental.

"You guys know that you don't have to hide anything from us, right?" I asked, mainly posing the question the Becky, but I let it hang in the air for a minute.

"Yeah," Becky answered, to my surprise, but I was starting to get used to her coming up to the plate when it was absolutely necessary, "You're right, Lyle. I'm sorry." Becky finally jumped from the table and grabbed the crushed bag with her. In her other hand she took Allen's hand, openly. "Well, if I'm not mistaken boys, we have a movie to watch." We all went back into the basement and settled in. The movie had answers. I knew it.

* * *

The movie was longer than I expected it to be, but at the end I sat there speechless. There was no doubt in my mind that Devils Tower was a place that could hold the T-Rex, and the clue made perfect sense. Larry must have assumed that I, or in this case Allen, would make the connection to the film and we would know where the last clue was. We sat there in silence to take everything in. It took awhile before anyone spoke.

I never realized how cool aliens were until I saw that movie. And Devils Tower was impressive on the screen. I could only imagine what it was like in real life. I understood why those aliens traveled lightyears to see it.

"Well," Allen finally said, "Do you think this is it?" I wanted to scream and jump up and down, dance, shot gun a Mountain Dew, or anything, but I remained poised and calm. Ellison was already suspicious, and I didn't want to add to it.

"The scene where the aliens arrive is very convincing. I mean, the tower is huge, both in height and circumference. And when Ellison and I did our research in the library it did say that the folded rock formations were a perfect tomb for dinosaur fossils," I said, sounding rather intelligent. "But we have a bigger problem than finally putting all the clues together. The fact of the matter here is that Karen already said no to us going to Yellowstone." And I was already at two strikes, but I wasn't going to tell them that and have them know that I was still being treated like a child at home playing T-Ball.

"But this is significantly closer to home than Yellowstone, Lyle. Surely Karen will understand if you tell her that. It's—what did you say, Allen, about an hour from here?—Plus, I want to take this moment to rub it in. My Devils Tower idea? Not so dumb after all." We all laughed. If only we had seen Devils Tower's potential sooner. Ellison really was onto something there.

"Yeah, that's right." I didn't have the heart to tell them that I was banned by both Karen and Dr. Calian from continuing the treasure hunt. I was keeping more secrets than one and I knew it was unfair to them. I was supposed to be accepting my offer from The University of Wyoming. *You're going to disobey my direct request of you working on this project*, Karen would say. *All for a dinosaur?* Yes,

Karen, yes I was.

"I actually think we should leave Karen out of this one. She has been under a lot of stress at work lately and has been manically overprotective of me since the incident with Derek. I don't want to add to that," I lied. If I kept them away from Karen and Karen away from them, there was no way that anyone would ever know that I was lying to the other.

"I have a solution," Becky said. We all looked at her in unison. "We take my car up to The Devils Tower the second weekend in April. My parents are going away on a Caribbean vacation and I wasn't invited, so they will never know." Aside from Becky sounding extremely bitter about her parents ditching her, she did present an optimal solution to our problem.

"That's almost a month from now," Allen said.

"Yes, but that's okay. It will give us plenty of time to research everything we need on Devils Tower before we get there," Ellison, always the student, added.

"This all sounds like a good idea to me," I said with a beaming smile. It was all coming together. All we had to do was hit the books and in about a month we would find the T-Rex. Everything would finally be perfect.

ONLY BECAUSE UNCLE
DANNY BROUGHT TURKEY

I skipped out on my Saturday meeting with Dr. Calian to go to the library instead. Dr. Calian would understand since I left him a voice message. I told him that I had an excellent idea for a short story that I simply could not pass up and was going to the library to work on it. So, it wasn't exactly a lie, but it wasn't the entire truth either.

The library was full of more people than I expected, but the directory was easy enough that I found books on Devils Tower in no time. It turned out Devils Tower was actually the first national monument instated by Teddy Roosevelt in 1906. This made sense because the thing was absolutely colossal. It only heightened my belief that there could one hundred percent be a sleeping fossil within its walls.

Most of the other facts that I stumbled upon were interesting, but not useful to my research. For one, the name was misspelled from Devil's to Devils. No apostrophe. Part of that felt like an odd sort of cosmic justice. This way the Devil was never owning the tower, rather it was simply its name. People can rock climb it. And the national park advisories warn against snakes, wasps, falcon attacks, and falling rocks. I wasn't sure which one of those was the scariest, but I hoped we'd run into none of those.

The most important thing I found out during my research was that since it was a national monument, it meant we could only stay within the confines of the park. So, if we were to find the secret passageway that led to the T-Rex skeleton, then we would probably be trespassing. Being arrested for trespassing seemed like a sure way to get the last strike from Karen. But, in this case, it was worth it.

I brought the couple of books I had up to the counter to check out. I placed them on the counter and the librarian just stared at me.

"Well," she said in an old croaky grandma voice, "You got your card?" I stared at her slightly confused. It was 2019, did I really still need a library card?

"Uhm, no ma'am. How would I get one?" She huffed as she turned her old creaky body around to grab a slip of paper.

"Fill this out and then come give it to me." I sat at a nearby table and filled out the form. It asked all the basic questions. I was taking my time until I saw Derek walk inside. It was the first time that I'd seen him since he assaulted me. And I wasn't looking for a second round in the ring. My handwriting became increasingly sloppy as I quickened my pace to fill out the form. I practically ran back to the librarian and slapped the sheet of paper onto her desk.

She was regarding it slower than a sloth, and I was starting to sweat. If she took any longer, I was going to end up in the hospital again with no chance at all to find the T-Rex.

"Good," she said, "Now, let me just print you a card."

"That won't be necessary!" I practically screamed at her, breaking more than half a dozen rules of the library. "I mean, just email it to me, I'll lose that one," I lied while snatching up the books and running. I could hear her yelling after me, but there was no way I was stopping. I had to get out of there. The handsomeness of my face depended on it.

When I finally got into the parking lot, I ran to Karen's car and leapt into the driver's seat.

As I was turning on the car Derek was leaving the library and walking right towards me. He looked angry. I needed to get the hell out of there. I tossed the car into reverse and slammed on The pedal. I took off at an inhuman speed going backwards, slammed on the brakes, shifted into drive and got out of there. While I was speeding out of the parking lot, I watched as Derek's figure grew smaller and smaller. When I could no longer see him, I finally felt safe.

When I arrived at home, I was stunned to see that Karen had gone from having secret diner lunches with Uncle Danny to openly inviting him over again. I didn't have a valid excuse to escape him again. I was already at the library "working on a short story" and there was no way in hell I was going back there to face Derek. The only option I had was to swallow a sort of pride I was holding onto and go inside.

Karen and Uncle Danny were sitting inside drinking coffee and were eating sandwiches. I was thinking about sneaking by and hiding in my room, but Uncle Danny caught a glance of me and called out.

"Lyle, you're home. Your mother and I were hoping you would join us for lunch. I got a sandwich for you in the fridge. I hope you still eat turkey as much as you did when you were little." Who invited that guy anyway? And why did he think he could just strut into my house and tell me what I should be doing? And speaking for Karen for that matter. But he was right about one thing. I did love turkey sandwiches. I casually went over to the fridge and grabbed it out before joining them at the table.

"So, Lyle, Dr. Calian called. He said you were at the library instead of his office." Karen's tone of voice was accusatory before I was even able to explain myself. There was nothing I could do at that point to satisfy her. That was what it felt like, anyway.

"Yeah, Karen. I wanted to get a jump start on some college work. You know, The University of Wyoming?" I smiled in spite of Karen's obvious displeasure.

"That's right, Lyle. Congratulations. Your mother told me, and that is wonderful news." I stuffed my sandwich into my mouth to force myself from rolling my eyes. *Since when did you care?* I wanted to ask. But the turkey was moist enough to keep me quiet for the time being. "How has school been anyway?"

"Good," I said before fully swallowing. "My grades are good, and I've been spending time with my friends."

"Still have problems paying attention I hear?" Uncle Danny's line of questioning was starting to get out of line. He may look like Larry, but he wasn't my father. And it certainly wasn't his place to criticize me after not being a part of my life for ten years. "Well," he added, "No matter, when I was a teenager it was hard for me to focus too."

I truly wanted to slap him across the face with my sandwich. If there was one thing I remembered about Uncle Danny was he always tried to make a situation about himself. Even the day when I went missing inside the tree trunk, he was complaining that he was going to be late for a fitness contest or some shit. But that was always Uncle

Danny. Self-absorbed and self- obsessed.

"What have you been doing in history class? That was your favorite when you were younger." I wanted to tell him that was ten years ago, and history was only interesting the first time you learned it, but I was watching Karen out of the corner of my eye, and I could tell she was mentally transcribing this conversation for her record books. She was a good umpire indeed.

"History is fine. I was working on a project with my group, but we are doing something else now," I lied.

"What project?"

"A county one, about Wyoming. We were gonna do something about paleontology, but that didn't work out, so we are gonna find something else," I said, carefully choosing my words so another screaming match didn't unfold at the kitchen table.

"What?" Uncle Danny's hard exterior broke for a second. His eyebrows furled awkwardly before he recomposed himself.

"Oh, we haven't decided on a new one yet," I said, stuffing the last bit of sandwich into my mouth in hopes that Uncle Danny would stop grilling me.

"No, I meant what kind of paleontology project?" I was nervous about answering that question, since the topic still felt sensitive around Karen. Plus, one mix-up and I could hint that we were still working on it and that would be the end of everything.

"Just some old T-Rex skeleton. Nothing too interesting, but that didn't work out, so no harm done, right?" Uncle Danny shifted awkwardly again. Maybe playing Dad was taking a toll on him. "Anyway, I have to go answer some emails about college. Thank you for the sandwich and honestly, Uncle Danny, you're not my father, so there's no need for you to pretend like you care about my education." I slid and escaped from there before Uncle Danny could ask me any more questions and before Karen slaughtered me for being so bold. He was being annoying and weird. At least Karen wasn't sneaking around with him anymore. That put my mind at ease a bit.

One thing ate at me while I continued to research Devils Tower. Larry had been gone for almost ten years, so why did Uncle Danny decide out of thin air that now would be a good time to reconnect with his family? And why did he think he could walk in and control the place?

Some things were never going to receive a proper answer. I had more important things to do anyway. I had to prepare for the trip.

WRITING IS HARD –
LOVE IS IMPOSSIBLE

The next week at school was more or less a blur of my own creating. When Metters lectured in the background about the red scare, all I could think about was Devils Tower and how April couldn't come soon enough. I was actually shaking in my seat. My legs fluttered in anxiety and I was chewing on my nails. If I didn't distract myself, I would pull my laptop out again and watch more YouTube videos of people walking around The Tower. I had already watched over fifty of them and I was starting to feel borderline obsessed.

I was trying to think of what Dr. Calian said I should do when I was seeing my daydreams. He told me that I should write them down in my journal. My mind had become so wrapped up in research that I wasn't seeing anything. Not a single bionic tree, fighter jet, or dinosaur was present when I looked outside the frosted classroom window.

Maybe Dr. Calian was wrong. Maybe I didn't have to channel my imagination into creative writing after all. Maybe all I needed was something else to distract me long enough to forget about how boring school was.

Irony slapped me in the face. School was boring, but research wasn't. I was spending too much time with Ellison. His nerd tendencies were starting to rub off on me. If I wasn't careful, I was going to start ordering lattes instead of Slurpees at The Mart. The thought of caffeine burning at the back of my throat made me shiver in spite of the cold. There was no way I was going to let that happen.

Maybe I should try to write a short story. It could be about anything I want. That was the beauty of writing, I guess. It didn't have to be right, but no part of that meant it was wrong. I pulled out my journal and looked at it. There was a lot of nonsense about the trees and raptors, but I wasn't sure how to turn that into a story.

Problem solved—I'd start from scratch. Create something in my head right now to ensure I would never pick up a coffee cup in my life. Okay. Attempt 1:

Little Billy didn't ask to be born with squid tentacles coming out of his fingers. Instead of nails, his tentacles would swing back and forth in the summer breeze bit by the crisp air floating in this ocean town in New Jersey. He often found himself stuffing his hands into his pockets to avoid the stares of curious children. He was still reeling from the time a child saw him and screamed, flailing his arms in a way that made Little Billy retreat in fear. "Monster! Monster!" But Little Billy wasn't a monster. He just wanted to be loved and run his tentacle fingers through someone's fluffy hair.

I put my pencil down and recoiled. What the hell was that even supposed to be? The opening to some sort of hentai porn? It was a disgrace. I didn't even know anything about New Jersey, how was I supposed to have a story take place there? Okay, attempt 2:

If there was anything I wanted to be in life, it would be a carrot. Buried deep into the ground, hiding from the faces of people. Just to be plucked one day and thrown into a beef stew. But, man, would I be delicious.

I wasn't sure if that one counted as a short story. It seemed more philosophical than story.

Carrots were gross anyway. Attempt 3:

There once was a man from Peru. Who fell asleep in his shoe. When he woke up with the worst case of an athlete's face, he scrubbed and scrubbed until his face was on the sponge. Now he was Spongeman from Peru.

It was trash. I wasn't even going to attempt to continue it. Why had Dr. Calian suggested writing in the first place? Just because I had a wild imagination didn't mean that I could translate that onto the page. One last time. Attempt 4:

The rocks under my feet were unsteady, but they clinged just enough to the soles of my hiking boots for me to pull myself up over the last ridge of the mountain. The air here was thinner, and my lungs refused to fill to capacity. If I were an anxious person, I would be afraid of dying. But I wasn't, and there was a sort of comfort in not being able to breathe correctly. It reminded you that every breath was precious.

The peak of my destination was just about two more miles away. My brow was still damp from the steep climb, but I was determined. The sun was high enough in the sky that it was safe for me to continue.

No darkness was going to impede my journey. I still had a few granola bars in my backpack that was now just starting to feel heavy on my shoulders. I was walking fast enough to feel nothing but my own determination. I had to get there, I thought, while looking out at The Devils Tower before me, calling—

"Lyle, are you even listening to the lecture?" Metters' voice caused me to stop my pen mid-sentence. Part of me was angry for him interrupting my constant flow of thoughts that were finally starting to manifest on the page.

"Uh, yeah. I was listening. The Cold War," I stammered. Becky chuckled behind me. I was going to have to scold her later.

"So then, who was the leader of Russia during this time period?" Metters gave me daggers, hoping for a reason to send me to the principal's office.

"Well, I mean, Mr. Metters, that is kind of a trick question considering there were two different leaders during the time period. It started off with Joseph Stalin and his legendary mustache, but Stalin died. There were some executions and ridding of people who were in the way, but eventually Nikita Khrushchev became the leader. And well, we all know how that goes." Metters snorted at my answer.

"Even though Stalin 'had a legendary mustache' as you say, he was still a ruthless leader.

Can anyone give me some examples of his harsh leadership regime?" I let out the breath I was holding through my nose. Good thing I have only learned about this war one hundred times.

I stared down at the short story that I had begun that

was successful. I subconsciously began to shift in The Devils Tower. Even when I was trying to force myself not to think about it, I still thought about it. Maybe my short story could be creative non-fiction instead. *A boy to man's journey about becoming the richest person in Wyoming for finding a hidden T-Rex skeleton.* I could already see it being a bestseller.

The only problem with that was I had to find the T-Rex before I could write about it. And there were still two weeks before our mission. The waiting was going to kill me for sure.

When the bell finally rang, I surprised myself by going up to Becky right away. I had to deflect my actions by teasing her first.

"Way to chuckle at me, greasy," I said.

"Please, Lyle. You deserved it for all your stammering. Plus, this isn't grease you savage, it's lotion," she said while rubbing it on her upper arm.

"Yeah, yeah. I know all about the layers of lotion that you put on." Becky and I made our way out into the hallway and continued walking to the cafeteria for lunch.

"Allen, I'm assuming?" she said, a slight sour tone spilling from her lips.

"Excuse me, but I never kiss and tell, Becky." She laughed now. A month ago, Becky probably wouldn't want to be caught dead laughing with me in the middle of the hallway, but there she was.

"Well for the record, I know Allen told you. Just an educated guess." Becky grabbed onto my arm which caused me to stop in the middle of the hallway. The look in her eyes was serious, and I was starting to sweat. For the first time in my life I wondered what would happen if she kissed me. "I want to tell you something, but don't tell okay?" She pursed her lips at me, and I was tempted to meet her halfway. But I would never do that because Becky was gross, and she was Allen's girl.

"Yeah, sure." I tried to remain calm and swallow the naughty thoughts I had just a moment earlier.

"I am going to tell Allen I love him tonight. Think he's gonna freak out?" I almost spit out the drink I wasn't drinking.

"Holy shit, really?" I couldn't contain my shock.

"Jesus Christ, Lyle. Have a little faith in me sometimes!" Becky started walking now and I had fully buried my thoughts of kissing her. Becky was in love with my best friend, and I was happy enough to come off as giddy. I pranced behind her to catch up.

"I'm sorry, Becky. I didn't mean to be insensitive, but you gotta understand how amazing this is. I mean, I have known Allen since he used to eat his boogers." She made a face as I continued. "And part of me always thought that we were going to end up alone in a senior center playing shuffleboard because no old ladies would want our geezer asses."

"Yeah, well. I do—love him I mean. And not all the fancy fancy, oh my God, first love bullshit. This is real." Becky's voice oozed with an infatuation that I hadn't heard on anyone's lips before. "But, don't tell him. Or I'll tell everyone it really was you who destroyed my bathroom." Threats aside, I had all of her secrets.

"Come on, that's ancient history. Plus are you really even that mad about it?" I thought of the actions that Derek took in order to get revenge on me for that, and I could only hope that Becky wasn't going to give me my second concussion of the year. The only reason why Becky even knew it was me was because Derek had to go and blurt it out to everyone. I was surprised she actually believed him though, especially after the live TV incident. "But I am happy for you both. I really am," I added before saying anything too gushy.

"No," she said while laughing. "I left it there for my parents to find too. That's what they get for leaving me behind all the time." I wanted to press her further on that because that was the second time Becky had mentioned her lack of a relationship with her parents. But I had already gotten one secret out of her today, and that was enough. "I am just really curious as to what you ate. Like, that was legendary."

"Karen's chili. It's amazing. You should try it some-time," I said.

"I think I'll pass. I have already seen what that can do to your digestive tract." We finally made it to the cafeteria and saw Allen and Ellison sitting together, almost as if they were waiting for us to arrive.

"But seriously, Becky. I won't say a thing. Plus, he's gonna tell me anyway." She didn't answer me; she squeezed my arm instead. And I somehow knew that was her way of telling me thank you.

We slid into the table together, the four of us gathered around our lunches. Our conversation ranged from how boring class was to how we wished it was April already. We all wanted to go and do this. If the world was fantasy, I would just fast forward to when we found the T-Rex and relished in our discovery. But I had to be patient and wait because our journey hadn't even begun yet.

* * *

Not so much to my surprise, my phone blew up later that night with a mass of texts from Allen.

> Dude. Becky told me she loves me.
> Is this
> real? Please tell me
> this is real.
> I have been dreaming about this since I was like,
> in the womb.

That's amazing, Al. I'm happy for you.

> Talk more soon, gonna go
> cuddle.

TMI. Be good.

And a final text from Becky that was short and sweet.

> Thank you.

Guilt began to surge inside my body for even thinking about kissing Becky. I wasn't even attracted to her, but in that moment, I thought about it. I wasn't thinking about kissing Becky specifically, more like kissing someone at all. Maybe kissing someone wouldn't be gross. Allen and Becky kissed. Ellison for sure was kissing someone. And there I was, the late bloomer, wondering if someone else's lips would feel warm against mine or if that was a myth created by movies for you to believe love is actually something special.

The glow of my laptop lit up from my position in my

bed and an image of Devils Tower popped up on the screen. I forgot that I changed my screen saver while diving into my research. It beckoned me forward and I obliged. No one ever said something about doing too much research. I opened a new tab on YouTube and searched more videos on Devils Tower. I could easily watch fifty more videos tonight. Anything to fill the loneliness that was scratching at my ribcage.

MURDER VS.
HAPPY BREAKFAST

Two weeks later, I found myself huddled over my backpack in my bedroom stuffing an extra pair of jeans inside for our journey. I wasn't sure that I was actually going to need them, but you can never be too careful. I read online that having an extra pair of pants with you is necessary because you might get wet or dirty on your journey.

That was how I had spent the past two weeks. Digging deeper and deeper into the internet. Reading blogs that people had posted about their trips. Reading reviews on Yelp. Hell, I even read about the history of the Tower before people came and ransacked it.

I read online that Devils Tower is actually a sacred place for indigenous people who are still living in Wyoming. The Tower itself is somewhat of a legend in their culture, one that they worship and idolize. The national park service even closes the tower in June to climbers, this way the indigenous groups have their sacred grounds to themselves. I understand why they adore the Tower. The history it holds is enough to fuel one hundred religions.

I hadn't seen Dr. Calian either. And every time he got in touch with me, I told him I was really serious about the creative writing piece I was working on and I needed all weekend to do it. He didn't know that it still sat in my journal as two paragraphs next to other short stories that were actual pieces of trash. He seemed to buy my excuse though and didn't tell Karen that I was skipping out on my meetings for almost a month.

Karen had been carrying on around the house like a phantom. She cooked, cleaned, and worked, but didn't say much to me. Sometimes, I would make awkward eye contact with her and force myself to look away. Her eyes always held a bit of pity mixed with anger, and if I stared into them too long, I might break.

I couldn't possibly figure out how the two of us allowed for our relationship to deteriorate so badly. That was one thing going on the journey might not fix.

The four of us decided, over a messy group chat the night before, that we would meet at Becky's at eight o'clock. That way, we would have enough time to get there. Becky offered up her car, but said she was uncomfortable driving for that long of a distance, so I agreed to drive us up there and Ellison agreed to drive back. We planned on getting back before it got dark outside. Karen was going on more and more of her "girl's trips" on Saturdays, so I wouldn't have to worry about running into her on the way out. The last thing I needed was to explain where I was going and why.

When I got downstairs, I heard a crash from the kitchen and almost crapped myself in the living room. Shit. What if Karen was here? There had to be a way for me to sneak out. The bathroom window upstairs was too high, and I would probably break a leg or something. Shit.

Why of all days did she have to be here?

I peeked my head around the corner and looked into the kitchen. But it wasn't Karen slaving over the stove. It was Uncle Danny. I wasn't sure if that happening was better or worse than Karen. I took another step forward that forced a creak out of the floorboards. Uncle Danny spun around effortlessly, like some sort of male ballerina performing Swan Lake.

"Oh, Lyle. Your mother said you wouldn't be up this early. I'm sorry if I scared you." I had so many things I wanted to ask him. The top of my list being: *Are you having an affair with my mother?* Uncle Danny looked at me and then to the backpack that I was holding. A gleam of recklessness in his eyes. "Where are you off to?"

"Dr. Calian's for my weekly visit," I lied, "but I am sure Karen already told you that, since you two seem to be spending a lot of time together these days." The second part spilled out of my mouth before I had the chance to think about my words. I came off as cagey and annoyed, which I was, but I didn't need him to know that. He took a few steps forward with the spatula in his hands oozing with the runny eggs he was ignoring. I wanted to run. In my mind's eye, the spatula was as good a weapon as a kitchen knife and I'm sure all the CrossFit Uncle Danny did would make him a tough competitor to fight against if he decided to beat me with a kitchen utensil.

"That's right," Uncle Danny said using the spatula to gesture in my direction, the eggs splattering onto the floor, "your mother did mention that." I remembered Larry telling me one time that Uncle Danny beat him up over an action figure they both wanted to play with. That meant Uncle Danny was ruthless, and he could probably tell my skinny ass was weak. "Do you want some eggs?" I looked to the floor that was now covered in them and imagined Uncle Danny smashing my face into the ground until I inhaled the fluffy bits up my nostrils.

"No, thanks. I'm not that hungry." My stomach growled in defiance, and I have never been angrier at myself in my life.

"Sounds to me like you are." Uncle Danny's tone had taken on a murder-like quality and I wanted to throw my backpack at his face and run. I wasn't going to let Larry's estranged brother step in and stop me from going on my quest.

"Nope. Just a coincidence. I gotta get going anyway—so."

"Wait." Uncle Danny was close enough to me now that I could smell the coffee on his breath. I swore his teeth were bloody. Like he ate the actual chicken for breakfast instead of the eggs. "Tell me more about the paleontology project you were doing." I was officially uncomfortable. I took multiple steps away from Uncle Danny and toward the door.

"I'm sorry, Uncle Danny, but I'm not allowed to talk about it. Karen and Doc's orders, so if you will excuse me." I ran out of the kitchen and to the front door. I grabbed my coat, not even bothering to put it on before exiting my house. I ran away from that house and Uncle Danny's bloody teeth. I didn't look back, not even when I heard Uncle Danny call after me. My feet crunched the hard snow underneath as I slid forward. The air was thin enough that it was hard for me to breathe. I didn't think it was possible for Uncle Danny to become any creepier than he already was, but I was certainly wrong.

I didn't stop running until I was about a block away from Becky's house. Finally slowing my pace, I slid my arms into my jacket and rubbed them. My bare arm hairs were frozen solid.

April offered no relief from the cold. I was alone for a moment before I looked over to see that T-Rex Larry had joined me.

He was wearing a jacket that was tailored to fit his T-Rex arms and a hat. He strutted beside me as the length to Becky's house finally came to a close. He didn't say anything to me, but I knew what it meant. We were closer than ever to finding the skeleton, and Larry was proud. Deep down I knew that.

* * *

When I finally let myself into Becky's house, everyone was slaving in the kitchen. There was pancake batter all over the cabinets and flour on the floor. The house smelt like bacon and cheese, and I felt like a cartoon character who rises from the ground to follow the pleasant aroma enticing them forward.

The three of them moved together like a machine. Becky was flipping pancakes onto a plate that Ellison was holding. Allen was in charge of making the eggs, which he was slathering an insane amount of pepper on. They didn't notice me walk into the kitchen. I must have been super quiet, or they were all just hyper focused on the task at hand—making the best breakfast.

That breakfast seemed a lot more appetizing than the one that Uncle Danny was making.

Something about his breakfast screamed murder and death, while this breakfast oozed the atmosphere of sunshine and rainbows. I almost didn't want to insert myself into the equation. I wanted to be the shy bystander who witnessed but didn't interfere. But I am not shy, nor a bystander. More or less, I am the entity that allowed for this breakfast to happen with my map and clues. I felt a pang of guilt for lying to them. They were going to hate me when they found out the truth, so I should soak up every bit of it as I could.

"Damn, you guys annihilated this kitchen," I said, successfully scaring all three of them.

Becky almost dropped the entire stack of pancakes she was holding.

"Christ, Lyle. What would you have done if I dropped all these pancakes?" Becky asked while putting the pancakes down onto the table and turning her attention to her fridge that she pulled a carton of orange juice out of.

"Simple, Becks, he would eat them off the floor," Allen answered for me.

"What's with the huge breakfast?" I asked, sliding into an unoccupied seat at the table.

"Well, everyone needs a well-balanced meal before they head out into the wild for a day," Ellison said. "Plus, we wanted to surprise you." I could feel my eyes widen at that statement.

"Surprise me?"

"Well, duh, Lyle, if you didn't get this project together, we would have nothing to do!" Becky said while finally sitting down at the table. Ellison and Allen followed. Everyone was smiling at me as they were handing out pancakes, eggs, toast, and orange juice.

They are going to hate me when they find out the truth.

I stared at the meal in front of me and I felt guilty for eating. I didn't help make the breakfast in anyway. Was it wrong of me to eat it? Almost reading my mind, Allen said—

"Don't feel too bad about not helping us. We all got together an hour earlier, so we could do this. Plus, you are driving the way there. Which is a huge help." Allen always knew what to say to cheer me up. "So, eat!" I didn't need him to tell me twice and I dug in. I slathered my pancakes with too much butter and syrup before stuffing them into my mouth. The syrup exploded over my taste buds and my tongue did a happy dance.

I couldn't remember the last time I had a breakfast like that. Probably when Larry was still alive. Something about that notion made me feel comfortable, though, and it was fitting. We were going on this trip for Larry after all, whether or not everyone in the party knew that.

I raised my glass of orange juice in toast. "Let's make a toast," I said, "For—" I paused. For what? "For— friendship." And for Larry. Everyone raised their glasses and we clanged them together. Yes, for Larry. That one was for you.

PLEASE
DON'T LEAVE

I pulled onto Highway 14, and all I could see were trees. The stretch of road in front of me looked like it could easily travel to the end of the world, wherever that may be. The heat was cranked up in the car and everyone was silent. Maybe everyone was as nervous as I was. I glanced over to Ellison who was staring longingly outside the window. I wonder what he was thinking about. Maybe *who* he was thinking about.

Just then, I heard the slapping of lips on lips in the backseat and it took everything inside me to not slam on the brakes and bottleneck into the back to see what was going on. Instead, I turned my attention to the rearview mirror.

Becky and Allen were all over each other in the backseat. Two horny teenagers so in love with each other that they didn't care who saw, or in this disgusting case, who heard their sexual antics. I tore my eyes away from the rearview and refocused them on the road. The slapping continued, and Ellison couldn't suppress a laugh in the passenger. It was my time to shine.

"I can't tell if you guys are going to frick-frack or if you're eating a hearty soup," I said as Ellison was all but rolling around in the passenger now. His laughing consumed the entire car.

"You're gross, Lyle," Becky said, pulling away from

Allen and buckling her seatbelt.

"All I'm saying is that it's unsafe not to wear your seatbelt, Becky. And that you probably should save the soup eating for later." I laughed at my own joke.

"Hey, look!" Allen almost jumped into the front seat of the car. For a moment I thought that he was going to beat me for making fun of him and Becky, but instead I followed his finger that was pointing towards the near-distance. "There it is!" Almost a mere blip in the distance was Devils Tower rising up far taller than any tree could ever hope to grow.

The GPS on Ellison's phone told me to turn on state highway 24 which felt like I was going further away from the Tower. I wanted to scream at the GPS for not knowing what it was talking about.

"Are we sure this is the right way?" I asked while slowing down the pace of the car.

Ellison pulled up the step by step directions and I watched him scroll through it in the corner of my eye.

"This is right. We just have to follow this road and it will take us right to the national monument. It does look like we are going away from it though, but everything is good." Ellison's tone was soothing, like he knew I was internally freaking out and was trying to calm me down. Highway 24 proved to be treeless with a house here and there. But the Tower did continue to rise higher and higher which eased my anxiety.

If it were a horror movie, we would hit a bear trap set out in the middle of the road and get a flat tire. I would have to pull over to the side of the road in a dramatic fashion. One that would toss around everyone in the vehicle. Becky would freak out on me for ruining her car.

When everything would finally settle down, we would get out of the car and find out that we were trapped. Before we could get back into the vehicle, a pack of diving falcons would come and attack us. But the falcons didn't work alone. They were trained attack falcons that listened to the commands of a hunter who loved animals but hated humans. An ironic twist of fate. And then we would become dinner, strung up over a fire to roast like a pig.

But it was real life.

I adjusted the radio station that fell onto one that was talking about the Tower. The radio guy mentioned that it was supposed to snow Monday, but that day was going to be beautiful and cold. He assured us that the weather shouldn't be a problem as long as you were properly dressed, and that not a lot of people would be visiting. That was excellent news. That meant less people would see us and become suspicious about what we were doing there.

We passed a bunch of posted signs stating that hunting wasn't allowed. There even was a sign saying "no fireworks" which made me think about which dumbass came up into a national park and thought it would be a good idea to set off some fireworks. You didn't put up a sign for no reason after all. I bet that person was a legend in their friend group. They probably threw parties for them to celebrate the badassery that came with breaking the law.

I could tell we were getting closer because we were near Devils Tower trading post that housed more than fifty motorcycles and a bunch of dudes and ladies sporting leather jackets. I hadn't realized the Tower was so popular among the hog riders. But they also didn't strike me as people who would be interested in climbing the Tower.

Rather just gather around in groups of five or six with a pint and talking about the one time they continued to ride into the sunset for a whole day straight.

The ranger station was up ahead, and I slowed the car down to talk to the lady sporting her ranger cap and green and tan outfit.

"Hey, kids. You got your ID's with you?" she asked while raising her eyebrow at us. I forgot my voice for a minute. Why would you need an ID?

"Yes we do, ma'am.'" Ellison nudged me. "Please tell me you did not drive all the way here without your ID." Oh, right. My wallet was resting in my pocket the whole time. I reached in and grabbed it. I peeled the ID from its protective clear sealing, and Pistol Pete, the infamous mascot of The University of Wyoming, stared back at me. A harsh reminder that I shouldn't be there. Allen and Becky passed their ID's up to me and Ellison handed his over as well.

I passed them over to the ranger, and she looked at all of them and then at us. Back at the ID's and then again at us. I was starting to sweat, and not because of the heat. What was she even looking for? Was she making sure we were actually human and not the aliens from *Close Encounters?*

"Would you kids like a map for your hike today?" she asked, rubbing her fingers along the ID's like a greedy fly looking for a new place to poop.

"That would be lovely," Ellison said eloquently and rehearsed, like it was the same thing he said during his Princeton interview.

The ranger finally handed back the ID's and smiled.

"Have a good time. The Tower trails are three miles

from this checkpoint. And remember to stay warm," she said ominously.

"Thank you for the tip," I said while slamming on the gas. Becky's car let out a squeal as we spat forward.

"What the hell, Lyle. Can you try to be a little more discrete?" Becky yelled. I was still sweating. My anxiety bubbled at the back of my throat causing me to have a lead foot. Allen put his hand on my shoulder.

"Lyle, it's all good. She doesn't know what we are really here for," he said as I finally eased up on the gas. I slowed to the posted speed limit of 25 miles per hour and took a deep breath. If I didn't calm down, I was going to ruin this before we could even start looking for the T-Rex.

Breathe in. Breathe out. Everything was okay.

I pulled into the parking lot and was in awe by the sight in front of me. The Tower rose in front of us 5,114 feet above sea level, at least that was what I read online. The trees looked like ants next to it. The radio was right too. There weren't many people there. The appeal of the Tower was apparent. Even without the alien draw, the sight that rose above us was beautiful.

My body put the car in park and exited the vehicle, but my mind was set on the journey ahead of me. All four of us trudged to the trunk of the car to retrieve our backpacks. All the while I did not peel my eyes from the Tower. I slung my backpack onto my back and took a long swig from the water bottle that I had in the trunk. I needed to be hydrated. I needed to be hydrated to start the quest, and to end it. I needed to be hydrated when we all became famous.

Becky slammed down the trunk of her car and we all started walking up the hill into the sparse trees that dared to try and cover the base of the Tower.

* * *

We continued walking for what felt like hours. The dead wildflowers underneath our boots were starting to make a familiar sound. The crunch and squeak combo somehow was soothing like rubbing together velvet between your fingertips.

I had the map out but quickly realized that it was going to be no help to us. The map was strictly a cartoon rendered version of the entire state of Wyoming. The X's all over must have meant that these were the places that the T-Rex *wasn't*. The only big landmark on the map that didn't have an X was Devils Tower. I was kind of mad that I didn't notice that in the beginning. We could have avoided all the videogame playing and arguing with Karen if we had just realized that the final clue was right in front of our noses the whole damn time.

"What exactly are we looking for?" Ellison asked while we all pulled ourselves up and over a steep hill.

"I'm not too sure to be honest," I said. The first truth to come from my mouth in months. "Maybe like a cave or something?" Becky said through sharp breaths.

"Maybe, but maybe not. When Lyle and I were doing research in the library, I read something about the rocks folding over each other. So, the skeleton could even be in plain sight. Possibly even right on the side of the Tower," Ellison explained as we continued forward.

"So, let's do a lap around the base then, see if we see anything in plain sight or maybe even a cave that we can slip into," Allen suggested.

"Yeah, let's do that," I said. I started walking around the base of the Tower counter clockwise to avoid the sun being in our eyes when we come around the bend. If the sun was in our eyes, it would lower the chances of us being able to see something in plain sight. Seeing something right in front of your nose sounds like it would be easy, but those are the hardest things to find.

We were an hour in and almost around the base with nothing interesting to report. Allen and Becky were starting to fall behind. Becky wasn't looking good either.

"Lyle," Allen said, "We have to go back. There's nothing here. Becky was stung by a bee or something and is having an allergic reaction." I jerked around to look at him in the face.

"We aren't done yet," I snapped. Allen was basically holding Becky up at this point. "What's wrong with her?"

"Lyle, Becky was stung by a bee. This isn't her fault; she just needs medicine." Allen was pleading at me with his eyes. He wanted me to fold that easily.

"Then take her back to the car and wait there," I suggested angrily. I didn't have time to waste on someone who barely wanted to be involved in this in the first place. Ellison stepped down from where he was standing next to me and went over to Becky. He started to examine her like he was a doctor, like he could actually give her a diagnosis.

"Lyle, she needs medicine. Allen's right. There's nothing here," Ellison said sternly. I could feel a tantrum beginning to burst out through my chest. But I swallowed it. If I were to freak out here, then all my secrets would come unraveled. And I could get the attention of rangers.

"What about the project?" I aimed this question at Allen, the only person in this group who knew why we were really there. The only person who could possibly understand why I needed to stay.

"You heard what Metters said when he gave it to us. If we find out that our topic is a myth than we treat the project as just that." Allen didn't mention anything about Larry. It was like he didn't even give a shit. That the girl clinging to him was more important. I looked out

past Allen, Ellison, and Becky, and I could see T-Rex Larry fading from the colossal being that he was, into but a tiny Floridian lizard. He walked away from the situation like he agreed with them. My hands were shaking from anger, not the cold. I sucked in a breath of cold air and released it out of my nose.

I failed.

I failed, and no one wanted to help me. "Fine," I said, "Let's get Becky home."

The walk back to the car consisted of Ellison and Allen holding Becky up so she didn't pass out. I trudged a few feet behind them, but it might as well have been a football field. I refused to help them. *An eye for an eye*, I thought.

When we got to the car, Allen picked Becky up bridal style and slid her in. She was pale and sad looking. I reluctantly got in the passenger and buckled up. Allen had rested Becky on his shoulder in the backseat. It looked like they wouldn't be eating a hearty soup on the way home. Ellison revved the engine and we started away from the Tower.

I continued to stare out the window ignoring everyone else in the car. Ellison and Allen were talking about something, but I couldn't hear them, and I didn't care. I watched as the blip that was Devils Tower got smaller and smaller, until finally I couldn't see it at all.

CREST OF
THE STORM

When Ellison dropped me off at home I went straight into my room. I wasn't in the mood to deal with Karen, and if Uncle Danny was still there, I would lose my mind. I laid on my bed and stared up at the ceiling. I could see every crack, blip, and cluster and it reminded me of the stars. That only reminded me of Allen, and that made me pissed.

I threw off my blankets, jumped to my feet, and paced back and forth between the Northeast Kingdom of my room and over to my mirror. I looked manic. I could see a primal glow in my eyes every time I made eye contact with myself in the mirror. My reflection was mocking me, smiling and shit, knowing just how angry I was. If my reflection was a real man, he would come out of there and fight me. Man on man, but he wouldn't. 'Cause he was a pussy.

Then I started to think about Allen again. Allen. When did Allen stop caring about this project? And why was he allowing a brand-new relationship get in the way of the friendship that he has had with me since we were kids? I didn't understand his train of thought. Becky was only stung by a bee, she would've been fine sitting in the car while the rest of us found the skeleton.

I didn't even know where to start with Ellison. One minute he was telling me that I could trust him. Then he agreed with them. They all just left everything in the dirt, and then what?

What was I supposed to tell T-Rex Larry the next time he showed up in my dreams? *Sorry, bro, but we gave up and left?* No. That wasn't good enough. Nothing was good enough and I was angry.

I picked up the pile of clothes on my floor and tossed it into the wall. The sound was that of a feather coming into contact with the ground and it wasn't enough. I wanted to throw everything in my room. I wanted to throw the bed. The stupid mocking mirror. Everything. Rabid yet controlled, my fist came into contact with my wall. The wall was stronger than I was, though, and fought back. All four of my balled knuckles cracked against themselves like a strike of lighting and suddenly my hand was on fire. It fucking burnt and I loved it. I punched the wall again. This time the crack was more imminent, like the storm was right above the room. No, the storm was inside, and I still hadn't felt the rain.

I punched the wall until my fist finally burst through and I could see the insulation inside. The fluffy pink cotton candy filling reminded me of Larry's body when he would come out of the shower without a shirt on. And there was something else. When I peeled my fist out from being swallowed, if I squinted my eyes just right, the hole looked like a T-Rex skull. The universe was mocking me.

No. It was a sign. A sign telling me that I couldn't give up. That the T-Rex skeleton was still out there waiting to be found. And I was the only one that could find it. It was dumb to think that anyone else would understand me. I didn't need friends—I needed closure. I was going to have to do it myself.

I paced again, and I could feel the blood dripping off my knuckles onto my wrist. I brought my wrist up to my mouth and tasted it. The iron was strong, and my lips were satiated. If that was what it tasted like to finally understand destiny, I would cut myself open and drink forever. But for a while, I was content. I was content with packing another bag. I was content with sneaking over to the bathroom to wash off my knuckles. The water stung the cuts and I could see the bones were malformed underneath my crepey skin. If I peeled any further, I would expose myself to my insides.

The mirror in the bathroom didn't mock me. Instead it was Larry, and he stared right at me. I could almost hear him whisper, *You are closer than you have ever been,* and that was all I needed. I returned to my room and continued pacing. There was no time for sleep. The storm continued to swirl above my head, but it was the only thing that calmed me.

* * *

When the time finally rolled around for me to go to school, I put on my best good boy act and went downstairs. I had to pretend like I didn't perform a ritual with my own body in my room two nights ago. Karen could probably smell that I was cooking up trouble.

I went downstairs to find her cooking eggs with goat cheese. It felt like an offering of reconciliation, but I was in no mood to repent. I walked right past the kitchen and went outside.

The air was crisp that day. The clouds above were signaling an actual storm. I packed an extra layer of clothes in my backpack just in case. I left all of my books tucked under my bed, this way Karen wouldn't be able to find them. I wasn't going to be spending too much time at the school today. I just had some things to say before finishing this journey.

The drive over was light and airy. Cloud nine must feel this way. I had never been in a clearer state of mind. No daydreams. No visions. Nothing. I knew what I needed now, and it wasn't my imagination.

I pulled into the parking lot and saw Allen and Becky right away. They were caught in a lip lock leaning against Allen's car. I parked a couple of spaces down from them and forced the car into park. Slamming the door behind me, I started over to them. I could see Ellison standing near the entrance of school with Derek and Chard. Great. That asshole was back too.

When I got up to Allen, I grabbed a handful of his jacket and pulled him away from Becky causing him to stumble. I readjusted my grip on him, so my hand was directly under his chin. I lifted him a little to force him to lean uncomfortably into his car. There were so many things that I wanted to say to him. I could see the reflection of myself in his contacts and I was wild.

Tears began to well before I could stop them. They streamed down my face as a waterfall blurring my vision.

"You—you left me, Al," was all I could manage as the grip I held on him tightened.

"Lyle, something's not right with you right now. You need to calm down," Becky said next to me. I snapped my head towards her erratically.

"This doesn't involve you," I spat towards her. I turned my attention back to Allen who was staring at me with the innocence of a doe caught in the headlights right before a sixteen- wheeler took its life. "You were supposed to be my friend. You were supposed to have my back, but you chose her." I pointed an accusatory finger to Becky who was now trying to pull me off of Allen.

"DO NOT touch me again." Then Allen lost it. He gripped my hands and flung me away from him. A crowd of students was starting to form around us with their phones out. That fight was going to be legendary in town.

"How dare you say that to me, Lyle? I have been here for you since Larry died and you know it. I have sat in every class with you. I have come to your house and hung out with you. I used to hold you when you would cry yourself to sleep when we were little, but that doesn't matter now does it? I was always there for you, Lyle. You are my best friend and I love you, but you are selfish. You never asked me how I was doing. Never wanted to talk about the things that I love, and how I want to be an astronomer. You only care about yourself." Allen continued to walk towards me as I let my feet guide me backwards. "I was the good friend to you. You never were a good friend. You're spoiled, immature, and stuck in the past. Larry isn't coming back, Lyle.

"*He's dead.* He's been dead for a long time. I know it's hard for you, but it's the truth. Capital T for Truth. You need to get your head out of the clouds and grow up. I'm not your keeper, and I don't give a shit what happens to you."

The tears continued to roll down my face. Whatever Allen was continuing to throw at me became inaudible. I couldn't handle it anymore. I stormed out of the crowd that was still videotaping us. I passed Ellison on my way to the car, and he grabbed my arm to try and stop me.

"Don't," I said. "Derek's back, yeah? Now you can go back to pretending to be someone you're not." I shook him from my body and slammed the door again. When I drove off, I could see Allen running after the car in the rearview. It was like he finally understood all the words he said and was regretting them. It was too late.

Snow began to fall lightly onto the windshield as I pulled onto Highway 14. I should have known from the beginning that it was something I needed to do alone. The letter was addressed only to me, after all. I was the only person in the world who wanted to make sure Larry lived on, and that was okay. Because I was going to make sure he did.

Soon I was doing ninety up the road. The only thing I could see in front of me were flurries and the future.

When we were little Allen used to wear the Batman shirt that he stole from me all the time. He told me we would always be connected—two heroes valiantly tethering themselves together.

But what happened when one of them became the villain? And what happened if you were unsure if the villain was really yourself?

REMIND ME OF
WHEN I WAS YOUNG

The snow continued to pelt my windshield as I pulled up to the ranger checkpoint at Devils Tower. I could feel the heat that I was blasting in the car turning my cheeks pink. My hands were starting to flush a glow of red as well as I gripped tightly onto the steering wheel.

My mind had not been able to settle on a single thought for the previous hour. A deep nagging was clawing at the back of my skull trying to taste my thoughts, and each time I tried to push it deeper, it came back up for another snack.

Was I really that much of a nuisance that no one wanted to deal with me anymore?

Karen, Allen, and Ellison had all called me immature, and Becky told me there was something wrong with me. I couldn't help but think that maybe she was right. That there was something wrong with me and my mental state was being buried alongside the snow that relentlessly battered my car.

All logic told me to turn around. The radio station set just for Devils Tower national park spilled out to fill the air and talked of snow over twelve inches—a rare occurrence in April. The tires of Karen's car squealed in defiance as I applied the brake to speak to the ranger. It was the same woman who saw me two days before. When I rolled down my window to talk to her I could already read the suspicion in her coffee colored eyes. I handed her my ID before she got the chance to say anything. She quickly glanced at it.

"Weren't you here the other day with a bunch of other kids?" I gulped down the little bit of saliva I was able to create in spite of my mouth being dried out by the heater.

"Yes, that was me. My friends and I were able to collect ample amounts of data, but I wanted to see how it shifted during a snowstorm." I bit the top of my lip trying to suppress a grin from my sheer ability to improvise lies on the spot. I was starting to get good at this. In a matter of time I was going to forget the truth myself.

"Shouldn't you be in school?" she asked, refusing to hand me back my ID while she interrogated me. Adults were starting to piss me off. I was eighteen years old, and yet I was still treated like a child. Still treated like a lesser because the term "teen" was still plastered onto my age. Part of me wanted to tell her to mind her own business— that she was taking precious time away from me being able to find the T-Rex. Another part of me wanted to unbuckle my seatbelt and lunge at her like the fully feral beast I knew that I could become. The storm from the other night was swirling in me still, and with just one switch I could turn this snow to ice.

The rational part of me decided to take a few deep breaths. In and out. Breathe in the stench of heat that singed my nose hairs in spite of the cold that was starting to creep in through the open window.

"School's closed," I said. "It's snowing." I made a large gesture outside the window to signify our surroundings, although I knew it was her job as a park ranger to be aware of the weather surrounding her place of work.

"Then you must know that it isn't safe to be hiking in this weather if school's closed." There was a hint of anger in her voice that I couldn't quite place. Maybe anger at having to work on a day like this instead of being able to stay home and curl up with a good cup of hot chocolate—or worse coffee. Maybe she hated her job. Or teenagers. But either way her anger was misplaced towards me. And, quite frankly, she was picking the wrong day to get on my nerves.

"Look," I said leaning as close to her as my seatbelt would allow, "I know the dangers of hiking in the snow. I have studied it as a part of my club activities, as I am sure you remember I am part of the hiking club in my high school. I just wanted to spend one of my rare days off doing what I love, ma'am." She snorted and handed me back my ID.

"Okay kid, just be safe and leave before the sun goes down." I snatched my ID from her and tucked it back into my wallet. In my passenger was T-Rex Larry, trying and failing to clap his hands together in victory. I had to stuff my face into my jacket to prevent myself from laughing. Then the ranger would think I was crazy for real.

"Thank you, I will," I said before rolling up the window and closing out the cold. The heat began to splinter through the car again as the steam rose around me in tendrils. I took a moment to let my body soak it in before gingerly continuing the three-mile drive to the parking lot. T-Rex Larry let out a roar that shook the car from side to side. His excitement only made me giddy, and I accelerated well over the twenty-five-mile-per-hour posted speed limit.

When I pulled into the parking lot, I didn't hesitate to throw the car into park and jump out into the snow. It was starting to form a thin layer on the ground, and if the flakes got any fatter, there was a chance that I would be stuck here. That only meant that I had to be smart and quick.

I was only going to search the part of The Tower that I didn't when we were there the last time. I grabbed my backpack from the trunk and settled into my gear. I put on an extra pair of gloves, another thicker jacket, and a hat that would protect my ears from the wind. I zipped my jacket up past my lips so the only part of my face that was exposed was a sliver from the tip of my nose to my eyelids. I pulled my hat down a little farther to lessen the exposure. The last thing I did was tie my boots tighter. I yanked on the laces to force them to stretch and contract around my ankle. I could feel the boot cutting into my circulation, but that was how I knew my ankles wouldn't roll in case I slipped in the snow.

Slinging my backpack on, I began my hike up through the sparse trees and towards the section I had yet to explore. The wind was resistant to me climbing up the mountain, but not even the force of mother nature was going to stop me from getting where I needed to be.

It didn't take me long to circle back to the place where Becky ruined everything. I could still almost see her clinging onto Allen hopelessly. The words that Allen said to me back in the parking lot were starting to seep back into my thoughts.

"I don't care what happens to you," he said. And he said it with conviction, with a seriousness that I didn't think he was capable of. He was always telling jokes about graffiti artists who drew dicks and pretending that he was actually drinking vodka. I thought we were on the same level. Or at the very least I thought we knew each other better than that. I guess I was wrong. I guess there are some things that you cannot know about everyone. That everyone is different when circumstances change.

True for Ellison who hid his sexuality and sided with Derek. True for Becky who didn't want to be seen in public with Allen until recently. True for Chard who faked unintelligence.

True for everyone. Probably even Derek. And Karen. Even the tightly put together Dr. Calian probably switched masks when he walked through the hallways of school in the morning. The wind bit at my nose once more while I hauled myself around the final corner. I squinted my eyes and noticed something that I didn't see before.

The snow on the ground was reflecting a shadow from something on The Tower, icy- white in the shape of an archway. I ran over, feeling my backpack clanging against me with each step. When I reached the shadow, I groped the rock wall in front of me, finding the opening. It took a few times before I was able to get my hand exactly where it needed to be. My hand slid into the opening in the rocks and I pulled. Small rocks started to fall around me one by one, and I realized this wasn't a hole. It was a door covered up by the rocks. I pulled them all out frantically. My fingers started to feel numb in spite of the two pairs of gloves that I was wearing. I got down onto my knees and pulled the last bit of the rocks out to create a hole big enough for me the fit through.

How in all hell did something like that exist without anyone knowing? Or they did know and that's why they covered it up? Larry must have found it and gone inside. The Tower itself was just a gigantic rock that folded after the Cretaceous period. It made sense that The Tower acted as a titanic tomb for a titanic creature forgotten by time.

I stepped inside to find that it was more than just a room. It looked more like a hallway traveling deep into the darkness. Luckily, I came prepared for this. I dropped my backpack to the ground and pulled out the flashlight. Switching it on, it illuminated the walkway in front of me. The hallway went forward and to the left. I followed it obediently—turning the corner close to the wall. Once I fully made it around the bend, I was no longer in a hidden cave in Devils Tower—I was in my living room.

* * *

I was eight years old and it was Sunday.

Momma went out for a girl's day with her friends and Daddy was in the kitchen making soup for lunch. He said today was going to be filled with adventures. He promised we would go in the backyard and look for prehistoric leaves that the dinosaurs used to eat. But baby dinosaurs, me, needed to fill up on sustenance before we would go on adventures. That's why Daddy was making soup. But he had been in there for a while.

The television was blaring with an action-packed show where jets were fighting in the air. Some war was going on, but I couldn't understand it. And it was boring. I switched the channel to *The Lord of the Rings,* which I never liked. It didn't seem possible for trees to come alive to me. The last channel I switched to had on *Godzilla.* I liked this one. Godzilla looked like the T-Rex from *Jurassic Park.* But *Godzilla* was almost over, and I was starting to get antsy. My tummy growled out, demanding food, and I decided it was time to check in on that lunch.

I hopped off the couch and pretended to be a dinosaur going into the kitchen. I wanted to scare Daddy. He would love it. I popped out and let out a huge roar, but Daddy didn't jump. He was sitting at the table face down in his bowl of soup, another full bowl across from him. I giggled. This was the most bizarre form of hide-and-seek he had ever played.

"Daddy!" I shouted. "That is the worst hiding spot I have ever seen!" I climbed onto the chair across from him and put my spoon into the soup. When I tasted it, it was cold. "Daddy I think you forgot to warm the soup up again." I dragged the chair over to the microwave. I stepped on it and put the soup in for three minutes. I did a little dance in front of the microwave thinking it would make Daddy laugh, but he didn't. When I turned around, he was still face down in his soup, not making a sound.

I jumped down and went over to him, frantically pulling on his shirt.

"Daddy, stop, this isn't funny anymore! I found you!" But he didn't move. I shook him over and over again, hoping that would wake him up. The microwave beeped signaling that my soup was finally hot. I ignored it and ran over to the phone. Mommy and Daddy told me if I was ever scared the police would help me and that 911 was their phone number. I dialed it and waited for a response.

"911, what's your emergency?"

"My Daddy fell asleep in his soup and he won't wake up," I said. "Is he breathing?"

"What?"

"Is he breathing?"

"I don't know. He won't move. I thought he was playing hide-and-seek because he does this all the time, but he always is fair when he's found."

"I'm going to send a unit out to you okay, sweetie? Can you stay on the line with me until then?" I could hear the soft hum of the connection of our phones fill the silence. I didn't know what to say to her. "Can you tell me how old you are?"

"I'm—I'm seven. No! I'm eight. I just turned eight!"

"Eight that's awesome! What's your favorite animal?"

"Dinosaur!" I shouted without hesitation. "Dinosaur's aren't animals, silly."

"Yes, they are!" Angrily, I tossed the phone across the room and it shattered against the cabinets. I went back over to Daddy and pulled on his shirt again. "I called 911 just like you taught me to, Daddy. I promise they are coming." I curled up into a ball around his feet and waited. I stuck my thumb in my mouth for comfort.

When they arrived, everything became frantic. They tried to pull me from Daddy, but I was trying to tell them that it was a joke. He was just playing a joke, and Daddy tells the best jokes. But they wouldn't listen. Momma stumbled inside to all the commotion and immediately was bombarded with questions from the officers.

"What is your husband's name?"

"Larry," she said. I repeated the name Larry in my head. "And what is your name?"

"My name is Karen." *Karen*, I whispered.

"And how old was your husband at time of death?"

"He's 35." Karen choked on what I could only assume was her own tongue. "I mean, he was 35."

"And did he have any known medical conditions we should know about?"

"He had high cholesterol and was struggling with his

weight. He was also recently diagnosed with heart disease. He is—he wasn't very healthy." I leaned in as close as I could to listen to their conversation, but I didn't understand what they were talking about, and I didn't understand why they were taking Larry out with a white sheet over him. I ran after the man that rolled Larry out.

"Please, stop, please! He won't be able to breathe if you leave that sheet over him!" But the man ignored me and continued to roll Larry out. Once everyone left the house it was just me and Karen. She was crying on the couch and I climbed into her lap. The TV was still blaring but now it was stuck on a repeating advertisement of the circus.

"Karen?" She looked at me with weird eyes that were more than just blossoming from her tears. "When are they gonna let Larry come back? He promised we would look for prehistoric leaves in the backyard." Karen adjusted herself under me so she could wrap her arms around my small frame.

"Honey, Larry—Daddy isn't going to be coming home. He—he is in Heaven now," Karen said, much to my chagrin.

"Heaven?"

"Yes baby, Heaven." I jumped from her lap and ran to go upstairs. I wanted to hide.

Every time I hid Larry would come and find me. This meant he had to come and find me right? Right?

"Lyle!" Karen yelled after me. "Lyle!" The more she yelled my name the more it faded into the distance.

* * *

I stumbled forward, not sure of where I was anymore.

I gripped the rock that was to my right, trying to balance myself and catch my breath. I swore I could hear Karen yelling after me, but something about her voice didn't sound right. I made a turn to the right which led me to a dead end. It was impossible. The T-Rex had to be in there somewhere.

I punched the wall in front of me, crunching further the bones that I had already been assaulting for the past two days. I brought the flashlight to my left and shone it on the wall. To my surprise there was a piece of paper dangling there. Upon closer inspection I saw that it was nailed to the wall, securing it in place for all these years. On the piece of paper was the troll meme in the shape of a T-Rex face. Two words were scrawled on the bottom— GOT YA.

My knees hit the ground before I realized I was falling. Everything—the letters, the map, the skeleton—it was all a lie. Every pain I had suppressed for the last ten years came crawling back onto me. Allen was right—Larry wasn't coming back, and he didn't leave anything behind for me. The screams start ripping at my throat automatically. A trained skill, just like how I reacted when I found Larry's dead body.

Everything always seemed like a game. But it was real life. My throat burned and was screaming for a drink of water that I didn't have. My body was numb and filled to the brim with dehydration. I pulled myself into the fetal position. I could die here for all I cared. Bury me here and create real bones.

Karen's voice rang out against the rocks again and I thought I was going crazy. I really was crazy.

"Lyle! Lyle!"

I couldn't tell what was the past and what was the present anymore.

"Lyle!" But it wasn't Karen's voice that I was hearing— it was Allen's. Allen rounded the corner with Ellison and Becky close behind him. Once he saw me, he darted forward, sliding onto the ground sloppily. He pulled me apart from myself and held me in his arms. "Lyle, why did you come here all by yourself? I'm so sorry, man. I'm so fucking sorry." Allen continued to hold me, and I pointed up to the paper.

"You were right," I said, "it wasn't worth it. There's no skeleton, guys. It was all a lie." I pulled away from Allen and looked at him straight in the eyes. His shone back at me filled with remorse and pain. Pain that I finally fully understood. "He's not coming back, Al." I collapsed into Allen fully now, allowing his body to engulf mine.

"We should get him out of here before it's too late and the rangers catch on," I heard Ellison say. Allen slowly stood up taking me with him. Becky looped another arm around my body to steady me.

"I'm so sorry, Becky," I said.

"You don't have to apologize now. You can make it up to me later, okay? I won't forgive you though if we get arrested here," she said while rubbing my back soothingly, trying to make a joke in spite of the situation. The three of them worked their way back out of the tunnel, dragging my limp and frostbitten body along with them. Soon we were met by the last rays of the setting sun.

* * *

Since we had two cars here, I went in Karen's car with

Ellison. He drove home, and I shivered in the passenger's seat. I allowed the heat to reenter my body slowly. Ellison didn't say anything to me, but I knew I owed him an explanation. I just needed to find the right words to say.

"Ellison," I whispered to get his attention. He didn't take his eyes off the road, but I could see him nod in encouragement. "I'm sorry." He turned slightly to look at me.

"What are you sorry for, Lyle?" he asked, gripping the steering wheel tighter.

"I lied to you and Becky about this history project. It was more than us trying to get a grade to me from the beginning." I hesitated, teeth still chattering from the cold that was enveloping my body. "The letter I found in my basement was from Larry. He left it for me to find with the map, but it didn't lead to anything. So, I'm sorry for lying and being selfish. I hope this doesn't put your Princeton application on the line." Ellison sighed as I explained myself to him. That was the part where he would tell me he didn't want to be friends with me anymore.

"Becky and I know the truth now. Allen told us on the way over. You know, Lyle, we still could have done this project knowing it was about Larry. I mean, it probably would've taken a lot of convincing to get Becky on board, but I'm sure she would've come around. You just don't put faith in people, man, and you should. We would've had your back from the beginning." I was starting to feel stupid. Ellison was right. I could've just been honest, and everything would be different. But we would have gotten the same results—nothing.

"All the people I have put faith in have left me," I said, honestly.

"That's not true either, Lyle. Karen loves you. Allen loves you. Becky and I, we love you too, and we haven't left you." What Ellison was saying to me was true. I had been stuck on the fact that Larry left me without warning for all of these years, and that made me afraid that everyone else in my life would do the same. So, I didn't get involved with anyone and I put my faith in my imagination that I knew, without a doubt, would never be going anywhere.

I fell silent and let the low hum of the heater fill the car. I was finally being hit by the exhaustion that was taking over my body. I stared out the window for the rest of the ride, watching as the snow continued to fall and cover the land that was once prehistoric.

* * *

When we finally got home there were multiple police cars in front of my house. No doubt, the school called Karen and she was freaking out because she didn't know where I was. I was preparing myself to receive the third strike as soon as I walked into the house. Man, I really hated baseball now. I didn't even have a chance the moment I stepped up to the plate.

Allen and Becky came to the house too. It didn't make a difference at that point. They have already seen Karen and me get into a fight, so what was another one to add to their resumes?

When I walked inside, the cops were gathered around the kitchen with Karen and it felt like the day I found Larry dead all over again. Something inside the center of my equilibrium broke, and I could no longer handle the situation.

Karen snapped her head over to me. Her eyes widened. I was expecting her to start yelling at me, but instead she did the opposite and burst into tears. She stood up and made her way over to me, and for once in my life I decided to meet her half way.

I pulled her into my arms and let myself collapse. My legs were finally giving out under me from a combination of the cold and stress. I let my own tears soak into her shirt, staining its light blue dark. There weren't many words that I could find. In fact, I knew nothing I could say would be able to fix everything. But I knew in that moment I had to say something.

"Momma," I said, "Momma, I am so sorry."

STRANGER
THAN FICTION

The beeping of the heart monitor I was hooked up to made me feel robotic. And not the good kind of robotic either, more like the artificial intelligence that is assumed to be hostile but all they really wanted from the beginning was love and affection, but they were killed in order to preserve the human race. The IV bag attached to my arm pumped me with fluids and drugs—ones that, without a doubt, were supposed to make me feel better. My right hand was in a cast. I broke four of my knuckles from punching the cave wall at The Tower.

After the entire Devils Tower fiasco, the police agreed not to press any charges for trespassing. I think they felt bad for me because I was in the late stages of hypothermia and the tips of my fingers were exhibiting signs of frostbite. I basically had to be rushed to the hospital. I was starting to get tired of that place. I mean, it was fun the time I came here because I ate all those pancakes, but that was because the nurses were talking about me like I was a legend. This time, when the nurses came around, I heard them whispering words like "amputation" and "coma." Those words were honestly scary as shit, so I decided not to think about them.

Karen stayed by my side most of the time, but I was usually pretending to be asleep. I didn't want to face her. Mostly because I knew the second trip to the hospital was going to mean strike three and I wasn't prepared for the consequences. I knew I couldn't avoid speaking to Karen forever, and I finally gave myself away when I coughed.

"Lyle? You're awake?" I was facing away from her, but I could tell that her tone of voice was borderline frantic. Maybe the nurses saying things like "amputation" weren't completely out of the question. The beeping continued to ring out, and I took a deep breath in through the nasal cannula that was driven high enough into my nostrils that I was sure the hospital was keeping visual tabs on my brain activity.

"Yeah," I mumbled, hoping that Karen might not have heard me. I could hear her shuffling behind me before feeling her presence lingering over the top of my body.

"I should go get the doctor then," she said, but from the noise I could tell she hadn't moved. As if she was waiting for me to add something else to the conversation.

"Can you wait a minute?" I asked. I still refused to roll over and look her in the eye.

"Okay." Karen moved back and sat down in the lumpy hospital visitor chair. I could hear the plastic crinkle as she settled herself into place.

"Lay it on me," I said without hesitation. I needed to know my fate now rather than later. "What?"

"You know, ref. Give me the last strike, so my ass can sit back in the dugout." I took the deepest breath I could in through my nose. I immediately regretted this though because I could start to pick up on hospital smells like urine and antiseptic.

"Is that what you're so worried about?" she asked. I crossed my arms in bed and pouted to myself. *Obviously*, I wanted to say. "Lyle, you could've died out there and you think all I care about is punishing you? What kind of mother would that make me?" I started to feel guilty. That maybe I read into this baseball metaphor too hard.

I had been giving her a hard time for the last couple of months, and I was sure her stress level was through the roof. The only thing stopping her from having a heart attack was her knowledge that I couldn't lose both parents that way. That's what I thought at least.

"You could've died, Lyle. You know that right?" Karen sobbed now. I heard her rustle into her purse and grab a packet of tissues. She blew her nose long and hard. It emitted a sound that reminded me of an elephant, and suddenly all I could think about was the day Larry died again. I didn't know what to say to Karen. I wanted to say: *I'm a failure, and I'm sorry*, but nothing came out. "Lyle, I don't know what I would have done if I lost you too," Karen added in between her stuffing her used tissues back into her purse and readjusting herself on her chair.

I took another deep breath and finally rolled over to face her. Her eyes were bloodshot and runny. It looked like she hadn't slept in days. It had been two. No, three days since I had been in the hospital now. The doctors wanted to make sure that my hypothermia didn't turn into pneumonia, and I had been recovering solidly. The word "coma" still made me nervous though. I could only assume they were talking about another patient.

"I—I just want to make you proud, Karen," I admitted, half because I was so damn tired from lying all the time and half because I was on so many drugs my brain couldn't make up any lies.

"Do you think you don't make me proud?" Karen asked. "Well, no."

"What in the world would make you think that, Lyle?" What indeed? Where did I even begin here?

"Because I'm a weirdo. Because I would rather be stuck in my own imagination all day fantasizing about dinosaurs and fighter jets than learning about Math and History. Because my only friend is a weirdo just like me. A weirdo who likes another weirdo. Because I am eighteen years old and still act like I'm eight sometimes. Because I never tried to get into college, and when I finally did, I didn't care. Because—and Karen I do apologize in advance for dropping this on you now—but because I quite frankly don't want to go to college. I hate school. School confines me. Because I am the worst son possible, Karen. I'm a disgrace. It has been ten years, and I still can't get over Larry."

Karen stared at me for a while as I awkwardly played with the thin hospital blanket that was equal amounts comforting and itchy. I couldn't blame Karen for just staring. Her kid was a weirdo after all.

"You aren't a bad son, Lyle," Karen said firmly. She looked down at her hands, probably so she could avoid making direct eye contact with me. "You have never been a bad son. Yeah you are immature, but what teenaged boy isn't? Yeah you hate school, but that has never stopped you from working hard and getting good grades." Karen paused and got up to join me on the bed. She pulled me tight into her arms.

"Lyle, I am so proud of you. And I am the one who should apologize. I should have searched harder to find someone for you to talk to after your father died. I was— no, I am a mess too, Lyle. I have never gotten over Larry's death either, and I never will. I have accepted that.

But you aren't a weirdo, sweetie. You are bold and bright and beautiful. You have the biggest imagination of anyone I know, and I promise I am not just saying that because I am your mom. It's the truth." Karen held me tighter and I continued to listen to her. I could hear her heartbeat through her mom sweater, and that was comforting.

"I'm sorry I went to Devils Tower alone. I wanted to make Larry proud, too. I wanted to find the skeleton," I said, deeply buried in the sweet scent of Karen's armpit by now. Ah, lilacs.

"Larry was and is always proud of everything you do, Lyle. Are you kidding? This is the same man who cried when you said fart for the first time." I laughed for the first time in what felt like forever. Larry did think farts were funny. "Lyle, don't ever change. Don't let that imagination of yours slip away. Yes, you have a lot of growing up to do, but promise me you'll never forget who you are." Karen was right about one thing. I never have struggled with my identity or accepting my weirdness.

"I promise, Karen." I finally pulled away from her and look at her for real. I was not sure when she started getting crow's feet at the corner of her eyes, or when the silver hairs started forming in her roots, but I was aware now that I had to love her harder. "There is still one thing that is bothering me though," I admitted.

"What's that, honey?"

"If Larry didn't leave me those letters, then who did?" Even in my drug induced state I had to ask the question. I had to know.

"I think you will get all your answers soon enough, but for now, Lyle, you need to finish recovering and get some rest, okay?" I wanted to pout, but I reminded myself that I was new and improved Lyle now. And new and improved Lyle didn't pout. He also needed to up the maturity of his jokes. Poop jokes might not cut it anymore.

"Fine," I said, "but only because the drugs are really kicking in now." I closed my eyes and let myself drift to sleep. A deep, dreamless sleep.

* * *

After three more days, the hospital told me I was well enough to head home. The tips of my fingers were no longer numb, and the inside of my body no longer harbored a snow storm.

I still shivered if I thought about it too much though.

When I got home, I went straight to sleep forever. When I woke up, I felt like Dracula rising from his coffin in the twenty-first century, confused about my where-abouts. I was thirsty as hell too, but for water, not blood. I gobbled up handfuls of water from the bathroom sink and let it restore my dehydration.

Then I sat on the couch and watched *Jurassic Park* on repeat. It just so happened that the SYFY channel decided to throw a marathon. It was like the universe knew I needed something to soothe my soul.

Karen was still a helicopter around me, swooping down occasionally to make sure I wasn't traveling faster than the speed limit. Well, in this case, to make sure I wasn't shoveling sour cream and onion chips in my mouth and that I was taking my medicine. She had to go to work, but told me at some point Uncle Danny would be dropping in to check on me.

I didn't want to see him. He smelled like pre-workout and eggs, and to be honest I was still traumatized from the murder scene he created in my kitchen before I left to go to The Tower. He was probably going to come here and eat me. I always knew he was a cannibal. It was the perfect chance for him to sink his teeth into me.

I thought about vampires and blood sucking a lot. Interesting. Very interesting. I had to write that down in my journal. I decided to start doing that again. It was fun, and I did miss my hentai loving character whom I hoped I could build into someone redeemable at some point. But who knew? Writing was hard.

When Uncle Danny finally showed up, he caught me with the bag of chips I wasn't supposed to be eating as I scribbled a juicy NSFW scene in my notebook about my two main characters having sex for the first time. The scene was starting to get juicy too. Baron was just about to slip Dolly out of her silky red dress. He came at the right part though because I had no clue what Baron was supposed to be doing next.

I expected him to come in and rip the bag of chips out of my hand and start lecturing me about health foods to be eating, including healthy fats like avocado. I never liked avocado, it tasted like I was eating a leaf. But Uncle Danny just sat on the couch next to me, which was awkward. I continued to shovel chips in my mouth in spite of his presence. I closed my notebook, so he didn't see the smut I was writing.

"Hey," I said with a mouth full of chips. Part of me wanted to chew them right in front of his face. Show him the greasy goodness that he had been missing out on all these years. But I sat there and behaved myself. What the hell was I supposed to say to this guy? Should I ask him about the weather or something? I didn't even know what he liked besides Crossfit, and lord knows I was not going to sit here and talk about exercising.

"I'm glad to see you home, Lyle. We were all really worried about you." Uncle Danny shifted awkwardly on the couch. It was good to see that he was just as wary about the conversation as I was. I swallowed a handful of chips too soon and the jagged edge of them scraped the lining of my throat. On top of that my mouth was dry from nerves. Uncle Danny did a little tap dance with his feet.

"Do you have to pee?" I asked. He looked at me with a weird face. "What, uhm—no, Lyle, I don't have to p—use the bathroom."

"Oh," I said, rubbing my throat for the illusion of comfort. How the hell are you even supposed to soothe a wound *inside* your body? "Sorry," I added before I shifted myself. There were so many things that I wanted to ask the man that was my relative seated beside me. I wanted to know why he stopped coming to see us. I wanted to know why now, of all times, he decided it was a good time to pop back into our lives. And most importantly I wanted to know why he was spending so much secret time with Karen. My curiosity scratched at my throat more than the chips and I couldn't not know anymore.

"Are you, like, canoodling with Karen?" I asked. There I said it. I couldn't take it back. "Canoodling?"

"You know—" Damn, I didn't take into account that Uncle Danny was an old timer and probably didn't know hip kid lingo. It was going to be much more difficult than I'd anticipated. "You know—like are you guys seeing each other?"

"God no," Uncle Danny all but cut me off.

"Oh, then why are you here?"

"I—" Uncle Danny stammered and the hard wall that he had put up began to crumble. I watched as he wrung his hands out in his lap, pulling on each finger individually as if to crack them. "I have been seeing a therapist, and he told me I needed to confront my past in order to move forward with a healthy future." I was shocked. A man as strong as Uncle Danny needed to see a therapist? I truly understood the meaning behind "never judge a book by its cover."

"So you didn't come here because you wanted to see me?" I asked.

"I've always wanted to see you, Lyle. It was just too hard for me to be in the same town that Larry and I grew up in. I didn't think I could stomach it. Seeing the place that he lived and died in." I stared at Uncle Danny as he continued to explain himself. "You know, Lyle, Larry and I were very close. Sure, we fought about toys and I would beat him up sometimes, but we were still close. We would watch movies together and play outside. We even would even make treasure hunts for each other and leave the clues around the house for the other to find."

"Hold on, what did you say?" I clutched the bag of chips tight enough that the knuckles on my good hand were white. My right hand constricted inside the cast, but I could still feel my fingers tense underneath.

"That we were very close."

"No, not that. You said something about leaving clues around the house for each other to find and go on treasure hunts. What do you mean by that?"

"I mean exactly that, Lyle. We would quite literally

leave the clues for each other that led to another clue, and another, and finally to a prize. Sometimes we would leave little figurines for each other, other times we would be more cynical and leave nothing, or a note with a funny face on it. We wanted to be adventurers, anything to fill the void that filled our mundane lives." I was speechless. I pulled the letter out from my pocket. I had kept it there since I found out it was fake. I was hoping that if I slept with it my dreams would give me the answers I was looking for. But the answer was right there in front of me. The answer was Uncle Danny. I read over the letter one last time:

L,

I know what you're thinking: How shitty of me to leave you a letter after everything I've put you through over the years. But listen,
I'm sure you're feeling antsy and are itching for adventure, so I leave you with this: you know historically that dinosaurs roamed through Montana and Wyoming. Their bones remain here. Particularly, the bones of a T-Rex. A full T-Rex. You heard that right. A full T-Rex skeleton in Wyoming. I want you to find it. Document it. Relish in the glory. You have the map. You have the mind to solve this.
The first clue: GO FOR GOLD. Good luck. You got this.

-D

Everything made sense. L never stood for Lyle, it stood for Larry. And D stood for Daniel. I had called him Uncle

Danny for so many years that I assumed the first letter of his name was a U not a D. I felt foolish for assuming that this was meant for me. I handed the letter to Uncle Danny who also read it. He gave me a knowing look, one that said one word and one word only: *shit.*

"This is the paleontology project you were telling me about, isn't it?" Uncle Danny asked. I held my head down and dragged my hands across my face. My cheeks were hot with embarrassment, and I was so ashamed I wanted to cry.

"I think I wanted to have something from Larry so badly that I created this whole scenario in my head without having all of the pieces. I just wanted to have something of his, ya know?" I admitted. I couldn't stop the tears now. They were dangling into my chips, which would make them soggy. Great, I couldn't even eat the chips after that.

"I'm so sorry, Lyle. I never thought you would find that. I didn't even know Larry kept that one. That was my last-ditch effort to try and get him to get up and be more active—to focus on his health for once. But it didn't work. He still died. And I always felt like part of that was my fault. That's why I left, Lyle. It had nothing to do with you. It was always a question of my bruised ego."

"You felt responsible?" I asked, still crying into the chips. Great there went a booger. The chips were soggy and slimly. Disgusting.

"Yeah, I was shoving Crossfit into his face and how well I was doing, and I think that made him depressed. Made him eat more. He was always an emotional eater. That's why when you were born, he and Karen had you on a strict diet. That's why you're all bones and no meat. They wanted to ensure you were healthy. But me, yeah, I—I should've done more for him than play our games from childhood still." If it were a movie it would be the part where I would forgive Uncle Danny and we would become best friends. We would go on Uncle/Nephew trips and everything would change. It would be like nothing ever happened. That he didn't disappear for years. But it wasn't a movie and I wasn't the same as I was before. And I didn't want to shut people out anymore.

"I wish we all did more to help Larry. I wish the last time I saw him wasn't under a white sheet," I said.

"Karen told me you've never been to his grave. You should go. It might help. At least that's what my therapist told me. I went, and I feel better." Uncle Danny was no therapist, and he and I weren't going to become friends overnight. But I had to give him the benefit of the doubt. I had to let myself heal too.

"You're right. I should."

"If I could turn back time, I would. I would go back and try harder for Larry. But the hard truth of life is you can't save everyone, and you can't always know the pain someone else is going through," Uncle Danny said while he patted me on the shoulder. "Karen asked me to stay here with you all day, but I think you should have some time alone." I didn't say anything, and Uncle Danny got up and left. Something he said to me rang in my ears.

You can't always know the pain someone else is going through.

I darted from the couch and grabbed my coat. Karen had the car, but I needed to get to the school. I needed to see Dr. Calian. There was only one thing I knew I had to do at that moment, no matter what.

MAKIN'
THINGS RIGHT

When I finally got to the school, I ran right into Dr. Calian's office. Class was in session, but Dr. Calian wasn't in his office. Damn. I needed him right then, but I didn't have time to lose. I needed to do it before it was too late.

I started to dig through his files and found the one I was looking for—Derek's. I scanned through it to see that my suspicions from earlier were true—he did lose his scholarship to Alabama. He wasn't expelled though, only suspended, so when I saw him on the day of the Devils Tower situation, he was starting back at school.

There was something else I was looking for in that file though. Something I was suspicious about but hadn't put two and two together until I heard what Uncle Danny said. And there it was. The part I was looking for—

"Derek wishes to apply to schools that offer rigorous programs in sports medicine and have an excellent football team. He wishes to be far away from home and away from his father."

The note was left two years ago by Dr. Calian. And Derek got everything he wanted—a school far away with a good football team and sports medicine. Well, he had everything, until he assaulted me. I could fix it, though. Thumbing farther back into the file, I found the phone number for the University of Alabama. I dialed them right away using the phone in Dr. Calian's office.

"University of Alabama admissions office, how may I direct your call?"

"Hi, uhm—I have to speak to someone in regards to a student who lost their scholarship—uhm, his name is Derek Sprout, he is from Harper K-12 in Harper, Wyoming," I said, hoping to sound professional enough that the mousy voice on the other end would take me seriously.

"Oh, yes. Him. He caused quite a stir in the athletics department. Are you the guidance counselor of the school?"

"Uhm—yes. I mean no! No. I am not, but I am the reason he lost his scholarship." I told mousy voice the truth. Lying had got me nowhere in life so far.

"Pardon?"

"Oh, right. I am the other student that he assaulted that caused him to lose his scholarship."

"Oh." Mousy voice paused on the other end, causing an ample amount of static to fill my ears. "Oh, dear. Yes, I will put you through to the head of admissions. Hold on." I listened to elevator music for at least five minutes, when a stronger more assertive voice came onto the phone.

"You want to change my mind about receding this student's dismissal of acceptance?" the booming voice jumped right in. They clearly prepared to be on the offensive. Little did they know, I had become quite good at baseball in the past couple of months.

"Yes," I said. Calm and crisp.

"Why should I? He assaulted you, didn't he?"

"Yes, he did. But it was my fault." "How was it your

fault?"

"I like to push his buttons. Well, I like to push everyone's buttons. I deserved it, quite honestly."

"No one deserves to be assaulted, young man. You better get to your point and get to it fast. I am busy." The booming voice was trying to be threatening. Trying to make me cower into the corner and throw in the towel, but I wouldn't. I refused.

"Listen," I said, stronger than ever, "Sure, Derek is a meathead and a bully. Yeah, he makes kids eat gum off of railing and he even put cottage cheese in my locker once, which was gross and really hard to clean up, but that's beside the point. Derek has a kind soul. Deep. Deep down in there somewhere. And all he needs in a second chance. I have learned over the past couple of months that everyone needs one of those sometimes and people make mistakes. But that doesn't make them bad people. It makes them human. And I think if you give Derek a second chance, if you let him come to your school and play for you guys, learn from you guys, he will change for the better."

The static filled my ears once again. I could only hope that my monologue was enough to convince booming voice to reinstate Derek. I heard booming voice click their tongue and sigh.

"You really think he can change?" Booming Voice asked.

"Yes. I do. I think he can. Even though he has been mean to me, I think he deserves this chance."

"Well," Booming Voice said, "I'll take what you just told me into consideration. This doesn't mean his actions will not still be taken into consideration as well. But I was interested in everything you had to say."

"Thank you!" I screamed before hanging up right away. I didn't want to risk saying something stupid to ruin all the progress I had just made...

BACK TO THE PRESENT

"And that was when you walked into your office and caught me with the phone in my hand looking probably guilty as hell. But that's the whole story, Dr. Calian. Every part of that was the truth," I say as Dr. Calian regards me with a stern look.

"I'm sorry I snooped through your files, Dr. Calian. I needed to call the University of Alabama and ask them to reinstate Derek," I admit. Dr. Calian has the biggest scowl on his face. One that says he doesn't believe a word I'm saying.

"Why would you do that?" he asks, pulling Derek's file from my hand. "I've learned a lot in the past few days. Can I ask you a question?"

"I think I am the one who should be asking the questions here, Lyle." This is possibly the angriest I have ever seen Dr. Calian. I can tell that he has had it with my shit.

"Does Derek get abused at home?" I blurt out in spite of Dr. Calian warning me against stepping over the line. Instead of scolding me, he just sighs. "I'm right, aren't I? I read somewhere that violence is a cycle. And I've seen him come into school with those bruises on his face. I always thought they were from football, but I had another thought. A more sinister one," I say, awkwardly sidestepping.

"The school has been looking into this for years, but

we haven't been able to find proof. Mr. Sprout is a very powerful man in the community and has gone through ample amounts of time to hide his actions. But yes, I believe you are right." Dr. Calian moves from me and goes behind his desk. He slumps in defeat. "I am very angry at you for going through my things, but I think it was brave of you to do what you just did. You must not tell anyone what we just discussed here. Go home and continue healing. You still have a history project to give if you want to graduate." Dr. Calian rubs his bald head in his hands and sighs. The end of the semester must be getting to him too.

"Okay, thanks Doc!" I say.

"Lyle, you better be on your best behavior from now until graduation. I'll be watching you." Cryptic threats aside, Dr. Calian has every right to have FBI-level surveillance on me after all the trouble I've caused. "Honestly, I can't believe that all of this happened over a bowl of chili and a note."

"Yeah, Doc. Me either," I say before finally leaving his office.

I need to get back home before Karen, so she doesn't start asking questions. I run all the way back and let the cold April breeze fill my lungs. Spring is finally coming. I can feel it.

* * *

When noon rolls around I am anxiously pacing back and forth in my living room like a shark circling its prey. I never thought that I would miss school, but I would do anything right now to listen to one of Metters' lectures on a war that I already know too much about.

The doctors told me I need a significant amount of time to recover. But I think I am all better now and would like to return to my normal life. Plus, since Karen has been in super mom mode, I haven't been able to see my friends. Well, I still hope that they are my friends. After everything that I have put them through, I would understand if they didn't want to be friends with me anymore.

I would understand, but I would be sad about it.

I take another lap around my living room when a commercial for the circus comes on TV. Larry always talked about taking me to the circus one day, but we never got the chance to. I think elephants look happier in the wild though. Wyoming Wildlife would be proud of me.

Seeing this commercial gives me an idea. I still have time before Karen gets home. I pull on my light jacket near the door and head outside once again. This time in the opposite direction of the school.

I am walking briskly, enough that my lungs have to do a little extra work. I walk around a huge bend and can see Chard's small home in the distance. There are a massive amount of windchimes hanging outside, and they are all banging into one another to create this melodic song that sounds both haunting and beautiful. I wonder if this is how Chard's grandmother summons demons. I see her walk outside and avert my eyes in fear that she will be able to gaze right into my third eye and soul.

I pick up the pace and turn another corner as soon as I pass Chard's house. In the distance, I can see the little bumps and grooves growing out of the earth. It's strange how one single bump represents a life—or sometimes even two when couples are buried together. The bumps slowly begin to take shape. Some are round, oval, or heart-shaped and stained pink, while others are more traditionally square, or ambitiously carved into the shape of a cross.

I have always been afraid of graveyards because of the one time I watched *Night of the Living Dead* when I was little. Karen and Larry tried to warn me that it was scary, but I didn't listen. I was six at the time and a grown man who could make his own choices about cinema. But then the zombies came on screen and there was something off about them—the way they walked, the way they didn't talk, and the way their eyes were filmed over in a sheet of white—needless to say I was scared sheetless (a pun I still savor to this day) and I swore off zombie movies for the rest of my life. I won't even watch *Zombieland*. I heard it's funny and I would like it, but it's a big no for me. Anything with zombies or cannibalism. I'll stick to my meat diet. Humans are gross anyway.

I finally reach the graveyard and see all the flowers covered in frost. People are dedicated to their loved ones even in times of cold. For a small town—a small state—a lot of people have died here. I am not sure exactly where Larry is buried, so I will have to wander around a bunch.

I take a lap with no luck. I take another lap and stop at the far end of the cemetery. It was dumb of me to come here without an inkling of where Larry is buried, and if I stay here past sundown the zombies are going to rise and get me. I start to walk straight down the middle of the cemetery but freeze when I see Chard coming in.

Chard is holding a bundle of pink and red carnations that he is clutching close to his chest. As soon as I see him, I dive behind the biggest gravestone nearest to me. I peek out the side to watch him as he comes to a stop in front of a stone shaped like two hearts.

I can see his lips moving from here, but I can't hear what he is saying. He isn't crying, but he doesn't look happy either. I inch forward a little and lose my balance. I land face first into a pile of baby's breath. Some of the breath gets into my mouth, and I am forced to chew on it to spit it out. It is unexpectantly sour and my face puckers up in resistance. By the time I am able to fully chew and spit it out, I look up and Chard is gone.

I let out a long breath. Thankfully he didn't see me here. I rearrange the smashed pile of baby's breath over the grave and quickly apologize to Mr. and Mrs. Abernathy. Just as I begin to stand, I look over to my left and down the row to see a small plastic dinosaur perched on the top of a slate black tombstone. The dino looks just like Philip—the plastic pterodactyl I used to sleep with when I was younger. I know this is the grave that I have been looking for.

I drag my reluctant feet over to the grave and take in the sight. Before me the slate black is filmed over to look brand new and shiny—like he died only a few weeks ago as opposed to ten years. It reads:

Larry
Farker
1974-2009
"Life finds a way" Rest in Eternal Peace

I immediately know that the quote is from our favorite movie: *Jurassic Park*. There is peace in knowing that he is probably still dreaming of dinosaurs too. Or, at the very least, he is a fossil himself now, singing forever.

I am trying to find the right thing to say, but I suddenly feel overwhelmed.

"What if he can't hear me?" I say aloud. I look down, and Philip seems to wink at me in encouragement. I turn Philip around on top of the tombstone, so I don't have to look him in the eyes. When I look up, I can see T-Rex Larry in the distance. He wiggles his little arms forward, encouraging me. I take a deep breath.

"Hey, Larry. Well, uhm, I—I mean, Dad. Is it okay if I call you Larry? I have been for the past ten years and I don't want you to think I am being disrespectful or anything. Uhm, it was just easier for me, I think." I pause and look to see T-Rex Larry still standing there. He blinks slowly. "Sorry I get so distracted all the time, my mind just wanders off into space occasionally. Well not space, that's for Allen, but you already know that. Remember when he tried to drag his telescope that was three times too big for him into our basement? He said that he wanted to be able to zoom in on the dinosaur scales. Then he cried when it didn't work." I laugh out loud at this memory. I had forgotten about that, actually, but I am glad to have remembered right now.

"But I guess I'm not really here to talk about Allen. Although, Larry, I am afraid that I really messed things up with him, and he's my best pal. I can't lose my best pal." I am unable to stop myself from crying now. The first tear slides out from my left eye and splatters onto the ice below me. It thaws it almost immediately. I can see a flower growing there in the future.

"I know I just have to apologize to him, and I will. But I wanted to talk to you first. I want to say I'm sorry for avoiding coming to see you all these years. I was afraid if I did, that would mean you are really really gone. Which I know how dumb that sounds, because you are gone and all, but I didn't want to have to say goodbye. So, I refuse to say that. Maybe see you later is better? Or something like that. Uhm, but I found your letter. Well, Uncle Danny's letter, and I just wanted you to know that the T-Rex skeleton isn't there. But I am sure there are plenty in the ground here. I hope you can hear them singing to you. And I hope you sing to."

When I look up again, T-Rex Larry is gone, and I am alone once again in the cemetery. I wipe my eyes with the sleeve of my jacket. I look down at the grave one more time and sigh. I tune my ears slightly and swear I can hear music. Or maybe it's just the windchimes. I turn Philip back around and begin my walk out of the cemetery.

Before I leave, I stop to look at the grave that Chard was visiting with the carnations on it. It reads:

Glenda and Archibald
Saunders 1970-2009,
1969-2009

They died the same year as Larry. I stretch back into the far reaches of my memory to try and piece together what I am forgetting. But my brain has had enough for one day, and I decide to continue my walk home.

The wind flips my wild hair in every direction and I try to smooth it down with my hand. I run past Chard's house in fear that he will still see me and wonder what I was doing. Once I get the momentum of the run I can't stop, and I let my legs carry me forward.

This is the first time since I can remember that I am

walking back alone. *But am I ever truly alone?* I think and continue running forward.

BOW-TIES, RED LIPS, ㎝ FLY GUYS

When I wake up the next morning, I have a text from Becky saying:

Meet us at the library—12 o'clock.

I quickly check the time and realize that it is already eleven and I am going to have to skip my live concert in the shower if I want to make it on time. I am also wondering why they are all going to be at the library when it's Friday—shouldn't they be in school? Well, I will just have to ask them when I get there.

I take the quickest shower of my life, throw on my *Butthole Surfers* T-shirt and black jeans, and grab my jacket at the door before beginning my walk over to the library. I have been doing a lot of cardio lately. I make a mental note to tell Uncle Danny the next time I see him— he would be proud.

When I get to the library, it is stuffed with old ladies reading murder mysteries and newspapers. I cringe at the sight of one old lady turning a newspaper, that is twice the size of her head I may add. I never liked newspapers because the ink would get all over my skin, and then I would touch my face and it would get on there, and I would look like a zombie. Not the zombies again! I really need to stop thinking about zombies before I vomit.

I find Allen, Becky, and Ellison in the corner with a sleuth of books opened, and a single laptop opened to PowerPoint. They are, no doubt, trying to squeeze-finish the project in time for Metters. We are going to have to come up with a whole new idea today. I suddenly feel extremely bad for not offering to help finish this project sooner. It was my fault that the first attempt exploded after all.

"There he is!" Ellison says with vibrance. I was sure they were all going to hate me. That they called me here and invited Derek in secret and he was going to beat me up again—this time for calling Alabama and embarrassing him in another state. But they were all smiling brightly at me, and for a moment I pinch myself just to make sure that I'm not dreaming. "Well, are you going to join us?" Ellison asks.

I didn't realize that while I was having my internal crisis that I stopped moving. I laugh to myself and whisper *Yeah*. I tentatively slide into the open seat at the table hoping that they aren't going to turn rabid and eat me. Oh no! My zombie prophecy is going to come true! And in the worst place of worst places to die—the library! I will be stuck reading Hemingway for the rest of my undead life! I remind myself to tone down the dramatics.

"Hey guys, and lady. Sorry if I am a little late. I uhm, had to walk here." I notice that I am doing a nervous leg jiggle under the table. Was now the right time to apologize or should I wait? But if I wait, are they going to think that I am being rude? UGH! The struggle! They are all staring at me too. I guess now is the time.

"Thank you, guys, for still wanting to work on the project with me after everything. I know we can come up with something better if we all work together." My voice registers as an octave higher than usual, highlighting my nervousness.

"Why wouldn't we want to finish the project with you, Lyle?" Allen asks while gently thumbing through the book closest to him.

Well, I think, *where do I begin?*

Because I dragged all of you into this project, lied to you about why I wanted to do it, made you sit in my living room while Karen and I had a screaming match, yelled at you guys for abandoning me (when in reality Becky was stung by a bee and I was jealous—jealous that Allen had found someone other than me to spend his time with), and on top of all of that, we now only have two weeks to finish a project that we have to start over.

My brain is on fire after thinking all these thoughts but forgetting to move my mouth to explain myself. Instead I just continue to nervously bounce my legs back and forth, two fish out of water.

"Lyle," Becky says, forcing me to tear my eyes away from the flopping fish. "We get it.

We all do. We know that you loved your father and that you miss him, and there is nothing wrong with that. I wish my parents cared about me like Larry did you. Mine would sell me off for a good vacation to the Bahamas any day." I suddenly feel like I understand Becky a little more. I knew her parents were rich, but I didn't know they always left her behind. "So, yeah. And I forgive you for everything. I don't like that you snapped at me, but I understand. And I promise I'm not taking Allen away from you." I look over to Allen who nods in agreement.

"Did you just read my mind?" I say without realizing

that it was audible. They all laugh.

"Well, let's just say it takes one lonely kid to know another," Becky says while gently resting her hands on top of mine.

Allen places his hands on top of Becky's and says, "We will always be here for you, man." I look out of the corner of my eye to see Ellison pausing. I can see the innerworkings of his mind churning a thought that he wants to say. I blink at him slowly, hoping that he understands that I am trying to encourage him. Slowly Ellison adds his hands on top of Allen's.

"My boyfriend is coming to the presentation of the project in two weeks, so we better come up with something good here." Ever composed and ever proud, Ellison's eyes begin to falter. But I refuse to let him feel alone. I feign surprise with a huge smile on my face.

"Well, shit," I say, "I can't wait to meet him. I gotta make sure he's good enough for my friend!" Ellison chuckles to let me know I was somewhat successful in dodging his embarrassment. Instead of questioning him, Becky and Allen simply agree, and we all mutually decide to go to The Rib and Chop House afterwards—Allen still owes me. No, I owe him. "So, let's really dig into this project then, huh?"

"I have an idea," Becky says, "And I think you guys are going to like it."

* * *

On Friday June 7th, two weeks after our meeting in the library, we all gather in Harper's small and stuffy auditorium to give our history projects. It seems like the entire school is here to watch a single history class. I am standing in the back with Karen and Uncle Danny, whom I invited.

It was a weird conversation on the phone with him, but I managed. I said "uhm" thirty- seven times in our five-minute conversation, but Uncle Danny ultimately said yes.

I am wearing a button-up white shirt tucked into black dress pants. I decided to wear a purple polka dot tie with it. If I had to be fancy, I was going all out. Except now the tie is starting to jab me in the throat and I don't like it. I dig my fingers into my neck and pull back on it a little to offer me some breathing room. Karen slaps my hand to stop me from pulling any further.

"Stop it," she says while readjusting the damage I had just done. "You look so handsome right now, don't ruin it! Gosh, Lyle. You even brushed your hair. I need to take a picture of this." Karen begins to dig into her handbag looking for the camera that she brought with her. Looking around, I see everyone else's parents are taking pictures on their cellphones. I guess that Karen didn't get the memo.

Allen and Becky start walking up to me as Karen says an inaudible curse word under her breath and says something about how she needs to stop packing too many lipsticks for one occasion. Allen and I look identical expect his tie is red. Us three gentleman may have texted in advance to plan this out. We all wanted to look dapper after all.

Becky is wearing a plain black dress with the doilies that Karen uses as a coaster as sleeves. Instead of wearing a tie, Becky opted for a bright fire-red lipstick. She pulled her thick blonde hair back into a sleek ponytail. They look perfectly fit for one another. Allen and Becky sway side by side in their couple swagger before stopping in front of me. I can't help but be insanely happy for them in this moment.

"Well, we are just waiting on Ellison then," Becky says flashing me her teeth.

"I hope he doesn't bail last minute." Allen raises his hand waiting for a high five. I give him a crisp one. "Hell yeah."

"Ellison won't bail. He's Mr. Princeton, remember?" I say laughing to myself. After all this time Ellison is still the biggest nerd.

"I was texting him on the way. Axel was helping him pick out his tie," Becky says while applying another healthy layer of gloss onto her already shiny lips. Ohhhh, she isn't sweaty.

She's shiny! I was wrong this whole time. And I guess Allen was kinda right, being that stars shine and all.

"I didn't realize that you guys spoke outside of project time," I admit as Karen lets out a frustrated sigh behind me. I can hear her slam her purse onto the ground.

"Well, duh. We are friends, aren't we?" Becky rolls her eyes and smiles with her fangs. "There they are!" Becky immediately walks over to greet Ellison and who I can only assume is Axel.

It takes everything in my heart and soul not to make a commotion right at this moment. Axel, Ellison's boyfriend, is wearing a crisp three-piece white suit and dark blue button up. His dark hair is slicked back and he walks with the type of confidence I can only hope for one day.

"Damn, Axel's a hunk," Allen says beside me, taking the words right from my mouth.

"Hey! From what Ellison says he is going to Princeton too, so let's focus on his brains you dog," I say to Allen which makes him roar with laughter.

"Woof." Allen puts his hands in front of his face and fake licks his hands. I slap him on the back of the head and walk over to introduce myself to Axel. Becky is happily chatting with him like they have known each other their whole lives, and Ellison awkwardly stands by.

"Hey, Lyle, Allen. Good to see you guys." Ellison rubs his hand up and down the length of his button up sleeve. I can tell that he is self-conscious about the situation.

"I see you went with the sea-foam green tie," I say, trying to lighten the mood. Ellison plucks the tie up and examines it.

"Sea-foam? Oh, I thought this was mint," Ellison says.

"Well, what the hell do I know about colors, anyway?" This makes Ellison laugh, and I feel mildly successful about the situation now. Axel finally turns to regard Allen and I.

"You must be Lyle. It's nice to meet you." I give Axel my best grown man handshake. "Yes, the one and only."

"Ellison has told me a lot about you." I suddenly get nervous. I hope that Ellison didn't tell him about the Devils Tower incident. If he did, then Axel is going to think I am an asshole and we can't have that.

"All bad things I hope." I laugh off my nervousness and point to Allen. "And of course this dog over here is Allen." Axel shakes his hand too. I am just about to ask Axel how his flight was when Karen shoots up and nearly screams.

"Found it!" She turns around and ushers all of us toward her. "Gather around here kids, gather around. I need a good picture!" She adjusts all of us together and even forces Axel into the picture. "Okay, okay. Now on three say, HISTORY! One, two, three!" We all mumble "history" unenthusiastically under our breath. "Now you guys better be more excited than that when you get up on that stage to give your presentation." Karen is being extra about everything right now, but I will let it slide just for tonight.

The auditorium begins to fill more and more as the time of the presentations get closer. Allen's parents and Juniper come in, and to my disdain June has a stuffed cockroach with her. I just know at some point during the night that thing is going to end up in my lap. I cringe.

Ellison's parents and his brothers come too, but Becky's don't. In spite of that, she seems really happy talking to Allen, Axel, and Ellison. I decide not to say anything.

The lights of the auditorium begin to dim ominously as Metters saunters onto the stage to begin his opening marks. He fumbles with the microphone that is attached to a podium with Viper the Viking on it. Go Vikings! A loud screech omits throughout the auditorium causing almost everyone to squeal in distaste.

"Sorry! Sorry! Stupid microphone just doesn't want to work with me right now." Metters twists and turns the microphone until he settles it into a spot right in front of his lips. He talks deeply into it now. "Thank you all for coming out tonight to watch the projects that my history class has been working on for the last handful of months. Can I get a round of applause for all of their hard work?" The auditorium erupts into applause. I am too busy digging my fingers into my ears to scrape out the noise of Metters' deep voice that felt like it was inside my brain.

"For those of you who don't know, I challenged them to come up with a historical project based on our county— Crooks. I wanted them to dig into a part of history that impacts them personally—a history that can be real or imagined. I am very excited to see what they came up with today!

Would group one please come up to the stage and begin your presentation?" Metters claps again which signals for everyone else to join in.

Thadeous, Aimee, Chard, and another student head to the stage to give their presentation.

We were given our order about a week ago in class, and to my group's dismay—we were last. That means I have to sit here all anxious and sweaty while pretending to care about my classmate's projects. I secretly think Metters made us go last on purpose. He wanted to get back at me one last time before I graduated.

Thadeous pulls up their PowerPoint presentation, which has an opening image of the infamous dick graffiti artist who struck in the 1980's.

I can hear Allen deeply sigh under his breath. "Humph," he mumbles while pointing to the screen. I can't help but laugh to myself as the group begins to explain the history of the most prolific character Crooks has ever seen.

Several painful presentations later, and it is finally our turn to go up and rock this room. I can feel everyone's eyes searing into my back as I continue onto the stage in front of me. I swallow down the bit of anxiety that is beginning to form as a rock in my throat. I remind myself that we all look dashing, we worked really hard on this project, and that once we are done here we all can celebrate by stuffing ourselves full with steak and potatoes.

I plant myself right behind the podium and Allen, Ellison, and Becky follow. I pull up our PowerPoint. The first image of ours has a picture of a T-Rex trying to clap his hands, but he can't because his arms are too small. I can hear the audience laughing which gives me the confidence to keep going.

"Good Evening, everyone," I say. "My name is Lyle Farker and these are my buddies here: Allen Parson, Ellison Jackyll, and Becky Road." At this moment, I would do anything for Larry to be sitting in the audience. I blink for a moment and open my eyes, but nothing changes. And I have to be okay with that.

"We have a treat in store for you today," Becky adds in a dramatic tone. "We are going to take you back to the Cretaceous Period, back to the time when the biggest reptiles on Earth reigned supreme, back to when turning a leaf into tea would probably kill you, and back before even human history. A history that lies miles and miles below this very auditorium. Because dinosaurs roamed here, once."

Dinosaurs roamed here once, I think. I look over to my classmates, my project group, my friends, and I know that we can do this.

"Now," I say, "extra credit to anyone in the audience who knows the scientific name of the dinosaur in our picture up here."

* * *

After everything is finished, everyone gathers in the auditorium to give each other hugs and praise for their performances. I walk around the room and pause at the top by myself to take in the sight. Metters comes up to me and awkwardly pats me on the shoulder.

"Great job up there, Lyle. You sure know how to work a crowd. So, I heard that you decided not to go to college." Great. Now I am going to be scolded by my history teacher for making an unheard-of decision. I try my best to hide the scoff on my face. "No worries, I am not here to lecture you about your decision making. I am simply here to offer you an alternative."

"What do you mean?" I ask, but as I say that a woman wearing an all-khaki outfit enters in behind Metters. She almost looks like she was bathing in dust. The only thing she is missing is a sack of tools to start excavating this very room.

"Lyle, I would like you to meet Dr. Marin from the Wyoming Dinosaur Center. She is a well-renowned Paleontologist and Archeologist. And I do believe she would like to speak to you." Metters creepily removes himself from the conversation and moves on to talk to another student. I don't even know what to say. How do you begin a conversation with someone you have never met before?

"That was quite a presentation you gave there, Lyle." Her accent reminds me of either British or Australian, but I can't quite put my finger on it. Either way, she came a long way to study dinosaurs. "I believe we may have a common passion," she says, trying to ease into this awkward conversation.

"You mean your favorite dinosaur is a T-Rex too?"

"Not quite, mine is the Pterodactylus, but I would say that the T-Rex is a close second." She winks at me offering a comradery without words. "Well, Lyle, I must say I have never been a woman of small talk, but I do have an offer for you. How would you like to spend this summer interning at the Wyoming Dinosaur Center, and if all goes well I can offer you a full time position on my archeological expedition to China in the fall?" I nearly have to stop myself from fainting on the spot.

"But, I don't deserve this," I say, almost instinctively. Dr. Marin frowns.

"Well, your friends seem to think differently. They are the ones who came to speak to me about you, after all." I look to the front of the auditorium and see Allen, Ellison, Becky, and Axel standing together chatting and laughing. They did this for me? I am going to owe them a lot more than some steak to repay them for this. I shuffle awkwardly and dig in to release my bow- tie from choking me.

"Well, I am going to have to get my passport," I mumble which makes Dr. Marin laugh.

"Of course, Lyle. All of those technical things will be sorted out, so you don't have to worry about it. What do you say?" What do I say? Easy.

"Although I disagree with your extinct giant lizard of choice, I am going to have to set aside our differences to begin a beautiful work relationship built on hard work and trust." I extend my hand and Dr. Marin shakes it while laughing.

"I love your attitude, Lyle. Once you graduate, contact me and we will set up your internship."

"Thank you." Dr. Marin leaves and I am once again standing by myself. I walk over to my friends. How am I ever going to thank them for this? They gave me the opportunity of a lifetime. When I finally join them, they stop talking. Now is the time to say something witty, funny, and sentimental all in one.

"Well guys, my wallet is sure going to be crying tonight after I pay for all our steaks." They burst out laughing. I have never been one to be able to voice my emotions, but I think they understand me right now. This is my way of saying thank you. "You too, Axel. Everyone gets a steak!" The rumble of our laughter fills the auditorium until it is the only thing I can hear.

PRESS
(RE)START

We all pile into Becky's car to head over to the Rib and Chop House for dinner. I told Karen that I wouldn't be staying out too late, and she bribed me to come home early with a surprise. She didn't tell me what the surprise was, just that I couldn't get it until I come home later.

She was all giggly and proud though, a mother truly proud to see her child work a crowd at a history presentation. She and Uncle Danny left to get dinner at the diner because they didn't want to invade our "teen time" as Uncle Danny calls it.

I was able to convince Karen to let me use her credit card to pay for dinner tonight though. My puppy dog face must have been strong because she didn't even question me. That or Allen, Ellison, and Becky already told her about the internship, and we were on the same wavelength about having to thank all of my friends properly.

The Rib and Chop House is a little way away, so Becky turns up the tunes and we all are scream-singing old things like "Call me Maybe" and "Teenage Dream," because let's face it—we are living it. The dream that is, kids. Make sure to write that down.

When we finally get to the restaurant and go inside, my nose is met by the sweet smell of deliciousness and savory flavors. My mouth begins to water before the hostess has even sat us down at the table. We all pick our seats and settle in.

I dig right into the menu (even though I already know what I am getting—NY strip, 9oz, with a side of mashed potatoes, gravy, and their sweet delicious buttery corn). I pretend to look at the menu some more when Becky lets out an audible huff.

"Sassy," I say, "can't decide what to order?"

"No, Lyle, it's not that. I know perfectly well that I want the grilled chicken," she says while rolling her eyes.

"Uhm, no. This is a steakhouse! You absolutely cannot JUST get grilled chicken!" I yell while slapping my menu onto the table for extra effect.

"Well you can't get away with not going to prom then!" Becky yells just as loudly. The entire restaurant is probably staring at us now.

"Allen, you told her?!"

"She threatened me with wet-willies, man. And you know how I feel about those so, yeah, I told." Allen hides behind his menu. "I think I'm going to go with a sirloin," he mumbles trying to change the conversation. I told Allen about a week ago that I was going to skip out on prom because I didn't have anyone to go with and I didn't feel like having small chat with Metters around the non-spiked punch bowl.

"You should come, Lyle," Ellison says. "Axel's coming too. We can do a group thing."

"I don't wanna be a fifth wheel though, guys," I say, pouting as the waitress comes over the take our orders. Everyone, including Becky, orders a steak. Once our waitress leaves, Becky looks at me with pursed lips and blinks extremely hard.

"Well, there you have it, Lyle. I ordered a steak, so now

you have to go to prom." I moan loudly to show my disdain with this situation.

"God, you guys are the worst. If I go to this thing and you bail on me, I'll find you." I point to Becky specifically. "And don't think I won't destroy your bathroom again." She laughs which provides me with comfort over literally shitting all over the place.

Just then Derek and his dad walk into the restaurant. I suddenly feel nervous. What if his dad comes over to beat me up too? The hostess sits them far enough away from our table, but still close enough that when Derek sits, he makes eye contact with me. He says something to his dad and then gets up and walks over to our table.

"Well, well, what do we have here?" I expect him to do something extravagant. Like pick up my cup of soda, dump it all over my head, and then proceed to rip open sugar packets to throw at me. The tiny grains of sugar would stick to my skin and make me itchy. But he just stands there, waiting for one of us to respond to his vague question. He looks tired. I can see the hint of a bruise yellowing on his upper arm. I cringe knowing the truth.

"Derek," I say, "I hope you have a lovely dinner. You should get a steak of course." Derek just snorts. He does an awkward shuffle but manages to remain intimidating.

"I know it was you, Farter," he finally says. His tone isn't accusatory like it has sounded directed to me in the past. Instead it holds a hint of something else—gratitude maybe.

"Is he still talking about the poop incident? Jesus, can't he get over that already?" Allen whispers even though Derek can still hear every word that he is saying. I want to fist fight Allen right now for becoming so bold. But Derek just snorts again.

"Anyway, thanks," is all Derek adds before heading to sit back with his dad. Part of me wants to invite him to stay here with us, order a steak and drink, and chat, but I know that the road to friendship with Derek might be unpaved, so I am content with taking baby steps over the potholes.

"What was he even talking about just now?" Ellison asks.

"I have no idea," I lie. Best to just keep this between me and Derek for now. I can only hope that him saying thank you means that he has re-received his scholarship, and he can go to Alabama and get out of here for good. "But, anyway, about prom. What should I wear?"

"Oh, ho. I can help you out there," Becky says while rubbing her hands together. "Prom is in what? One week? Then we graduate. Feels like this flew by."

"Alright, now. Let's not get all misty eyed over a delicious meal here. We can save the tears for our diplomas," I say just in time for our steaks to be delivered to our table. We all dig in and continue to chat about everything and anything.

Axel talks about looking forward to moving to New Jersey with Ellison in August. Becky and Allen both decided to stay local-ish. They are going to the west coast to study at The University of Oregon. Allen was able to get a pretty hefty scholarship to go, and Becky was more than happy to bop out of Wyoming with him.

As for me, I am going to stick around her for a bit. See where this internship goes. And hopefully in the fall I will be starting a new adventure. I can see my story coming together with a nice bow, but there is something that is still bothering me.

"Hey, you guys know why Chard was at the graveyard the other day?" I ask, trying my best to sound casual and not like I am probing for answers to something that has been eating at me for weeks.

"Pretty sure he still goes once a week, for his parents ya know?" Ellison says in between big gulps of his soda.

"His parents?" The confusion on my face must be prevalent because everyone except Axel looks at me funny.

"Oh, true. You probably don't remember because they died the same year as Larry. Bad car accident in the snow. He took a whole year off to recover, but I heard he got into The University of Wyoming, so he will be good," Ellison adds nonchalantly. But to me this is huge. And all those times I made fun of him for being dumb. Man. His grandma probably isn't even a witch. I have been so wrong about so many things. Before I have an existential crisis over a hunk of meat, I decide to change the subject.

"This steak is moist," I say taking another big bite.

"Gross, Lyle! Why couldn't you call it something else?!" Becky throws a napkin at me.

"What's wrong with the word moist?" I ask, playing coy and batting my eyelashes. "You're nasty. Just eat your steak and keep your adjectives to yourself." Even though she is being harsh, she still laughs. Not my fault the steak is delicious. Sue me. I wolf down the rest of my steak and breathe in every word that my friends are saying, taking mental notes of each of their mannerisms. In one week there will be prom. Another two after that we graduate. And then—stay tuned.

Becky drops me off at my house after we finish up dinner and I pay for everyone's steaks using Karen's credit card. When I come into the house, I find Karen sitting in the kitchen. She is sipping on a cup of tea and reading a book about a woman who snapped and killed her husband. Not sure why every mom is obsessed with murder, but I am too afraid to question it.

In front of Karen is a present wrapped in blue with a fat bow on it. I join Karen at the table, eager to see what she has in store for me.

The battleground of the kitchen table has thus become a ground for ceasefire. One where we can sign a treaty of peace. One where we can eat dinner and not have to worry about screaming at one another anymore. But more than any of that, it is sacred grounds. The last place where Larry was alive.

"How was dinner?" Karen asks, taking another sip of her tea.

"It was great, everyone enjoyed their steaks. Mine was moist and succulent."

"Moist? Isn't that more a way to explain a cake?" What's with everyone not liking the word moist? What can I say? It has a nice ring to it.

"Maybe, but I think I just wanted to push Becky's buttons. Speaking of, I have decided that I am going to prom, so we are gonna have to go tux shopping." Karen's eyes widen in disbelief.

"What made you decide that?"

"Well, I figured that you only get to grind on your classmates in a sweaty gym once in your life, so I might as well take up that opportunity." I smile. No way am I going to tell Karen that I was essentially bribed into going.

"Well I certainly hope that you won't be grinding on anyone. But I am glad you decided to go." Karen slides the present sitting on the table closer to me. "This is for you. A gift for putting on an amazing presentation." I pick up the gift and give it a little shake. It rumbles inside, a beast in a cage that wants to be set free.

I tear into the gift and pause when I see what it is—the 25th anniversary collection of *Jurassic Park*. It has all the movies in it.

"I know how you feel about the original VHS in the basement, but I thought it was time to get you a new one. Plus, I don't think you are going to find many VHS players in China." I can see Karen's eyes becoming misty. I swallow down the tears threatening to spill themselves. It turns out that Karen and I were actually on the same baseball team the whole time.

"You are right, I don't think that I will find any VHS players in China." I get up from my chair and give Karen a big hug. "Thank you for this. I know you know how much this means to me."

"Of course. And never forget how proud I am. Larry too. If he could see you now—" Karen doesn't finish her thought, but she doesn't need to. She has said enough to fill my heart with gratitude. I sit back down for a bit and talk to Karen about all my friends' plans for college until she excuses herself to go to bed.

Once Karen leaves, I sneak into the basement. Everything is the same since Allen and I came down here. It is a little chilly and dusty, but I shake that off. I pull the protective sealing off of my new gift. When I pop the case open, the first movie is the original *Jurassic Park*—exactly where it is intended to be.

For a moment I am eight again. I am dancing around my basement in my Batman undies and stuffing my mouth with sour cream and onion chips—the crumbs always used to get stuck in my butt crack. Allen is mumbling in the corner about wanting more pizza, and Larry is sloshing around pretending to be a dinosaur.

In real time, I slide the DVD into the player and wait for the play screen to come on. I feel I have changed, but I still am me, inherently. I still am going to see fighter jets and bionic trees. I am still going to live inside my head at times. And although I won't see Larry anymore, I know he is always here with me.

If there is any place in the world that I could be stuck forever it would be in the wilds of my own imagination, and I am at peace with that.

The play screen flashes on the TV and I grab the remote. I take a deep breath and close my eyes for a moment. Everything in my life is about to change. But for now, the only thing I am concerned with is pressing play.

ACKNOWLEDGEMENTS

This book has been a crazy ride, and without the help of so many people, it would not exist at all. To my lovely editor, Trista, thank you for taking this on, believing in it, and giving me the confidence to put it out into the world. To Nick, thank you for believing in Lyle as well and adding it to your amazing line up at Atmosphere. And to Atmosphere Press for giving my novel a home.

For my VCFA family, who saw this novel through many iterations--including a wild screenplay. Erin and Jordan, thank you for reading, editing, and encouraging me to keep going, no matter what.

For my Mom and Dad, who always, always encouraged me to follow my dreams and bought me those plastic dinosaurs that I never (and will never) forget.

For my brother, who gave me a lot of source material into the mind of a teenage boy (poop jokes and all) and who has always, mercilessly been himself.

For Josh, who cried with me when my novel got accepted, but also--for never letting me give up.

For the cat, who always sat on the desk with me and had a keen eye for any mistakes.

ABOUT
ATMOSPHERE PRESS

Atmosphere Press is an independent, full-service publisher for excellent books in all genres and for all audiences. Learn more about what we do at atmospherepress.com.

We encourage you to check out some of Atmosphere's latest releases, which are available at Amazon.com and via order from your local bookstore:

The Embers of Tradition, a novel by Chukwudum Okeke

Saints and Martyrs: A Novel, by Aaron Roe

When I Am Ashes, a novel by Amber Rose

Melancholy Vision: A Revolution Series Novel, by L.C. Hamilton

The Recoleta Stories, by Bryon Esmond Butler

Voodoo Hideaway, a novel by Vance Cariaga

Hart Street and Main, a novel by Tabitha Sprunger

The Weed Lady, a novel by Shea R. Embry

A Book of Life, a novel by David Ellis

It Was Called a Home, a novel by Brian Nisun

Grace, a novel by Nancy Allen

Shifted, a novel by KristaLyn A. Vetovich

ABOUT
THE AUTHOR

Kayleigh Marinelli is a writer of stories that blur the lines of reality. She has been writing stories about ghosts and dinosaurs since she was young. Now, she writes stories about ghosts, dinosaurs, and the human experience. *The Fantastic Fabricated Life of Lyle Farker* is her debut novel. She can usually be found reading, eating, or teaching in New York with her partner and sweet black cat, Orion.

CPSIA information can be obtained
at www.ICGtesting.com
Printed in the USA
LVHW090900171221
706233LV00005B/263